B.D.PEDERSEN

I0679143

TIME TRAP

Edited
by
June Pedersen

ISBN-13: 978-0692564608
ISBN-10: 0692564608

PROLOGUE

Time is a process each and every one of us is a slave to. Time is a measurement of one's movement through a sequence of events that make up what we refer to as our lives.

We only really become aware of time and its impact on us when we become more aware of the world around us. As a new child, time has no meaning and we have no fundamental grasp as to what it is or what it means.

As we grow older, a measurement of time, we become more aware of time and the value we come to place on it. But what if you could control time? What if you could take time and manipulate it in any manner you wanted for as long as you wanted? What if, while in this game of time manipulation, you find there are hidden traps, hidden spots in time you have no control over?

Yeah, what if, I don't think that either you or I really know or understand what time is and where time came from. We see time from a highly restricted perspective, our own lives. We see time as an element of our life that is always slipping away from us. Always moving us along in this place, this space we live in.

It robs us of our youth and steals precious moments and seconds in each day as we try to negotiate this time space thing and do so with as little use of time as we can.

What the hell am I saying anyway? I guess I'm trying to tell you time, all times are important. All we do is based on time and when someone, anyone discovers they can manipulate time that is a real threat to you and all you know and hold dear.

Can time be manipulated? There is a hint that it can because it does strange things all on its own. For example; have you ever looked down on your wrist watch and at that moment, as you focus on the face of the watch it appears the second hand just started to move? For that instant when you looked down it appears the second hand is motionless and then it starts to move.

Is that real? Is the watch actually starting up when you look at it and focus on it? It sure as hell looks like it, but is it? Who knows what the answer is to that question and a number of others as well. Time is an enigma, a force of nature no one really knows or understands. Our hero is no different.

David Jacobs will learn that lesson, in spades. One lapse of judgment, one moment of indecision and time can be totally screwed up. Not just for you but for everyone around you, everyone that you hold dear.

One moment of fear and denial and David sent his dearest friend into a place no man ever deserves to go. Out of that would come Time Trap and that weapon would be used on David. He would experience the most hellish of events any one person could ever experience and all because of fear and a failure to act.

He would find himself in a place, a time when his children would be older than he was. Where his entire life had been turned upside down, only to discover he must face the revenge of the one he betrayed.

Albert Aberdeen would disappear one day and some thirty years later come back into David's life in a way no man could anticipate. With Albert's reappearance David would be faced with the single most difficult decision of his life. A decision that would carry an impact over a thirty-year period in which even the world would face total and complete annihilation.

When time is manipulated and people are targeted there can be only one resulting consequence. Someone, somewhere, is going to pay. Someone, somewhere, had used time as a separator from his current time and that time when he carried out his despicable act. But when time can be manipulated, that someone can be placed right back into a point in time when they made the fatal decision, and be forced to re-live it.

It would all start out on a beautiful summer day. A simple trip to the post office would turn into a nightmare and the plans of everyone David had ever been in contact with would be changed and intermingled creating a death dance that some would survive and others would not.

David would find himself striving to regain the moment in time when all changed, when one's actions and decisions from the past reach into the future and dragged them back to a time, in the past to be faced all over again.

CHAPTER ONE

The Return

How do I start this? How do I even begin to explain what I know has happened to me? How do I say I had been gone for thirty years and yet I appeared to have not aged one day?

Hell, I didn't even have the answers to those questions. How did they expect me to tell them anything? All I know is I left the house one day and no one saw me again until ten hours ago. Damn, listen to me. I walked out the back door and got in my car. All I had to do was drive down to the post office and send off a package.

To me I did just that. I backed out of the driveway and then headed into town. I got to the post office and sent the package and, oh yes, two letters also and returned to my car and headed back home.

During that time nothing happened. When I got home, I found everything had changed. No one I knew was there and as I tried to enter the back door, whoever was in the house called the police. When they arrived, they arrested me and here I am.

As the officers approached me, they stopped and looked at my car, a 2015 Buick 4 door. One of them wrote the license number down and then asked for my driver's license, which I handed over to them. The first thing the one officer asked me was whether I knew my license was expired and it had been since 2016.

That stopped me short. "What do you mean 2016?"

The officers stood there looking at me, and then the one holding the license leaned over. "Mr. Jacobs, this license has been expired for twenty-nine years. Sir, this is 2045."

I guess that's when I passed out. Next thing I know I'm in the back of a patrol car watching a tow truck hauling my car away. As the officer got back into the patrol car I asked. "What are you going to do with my car?" I had a feeling I was about to become part of something only hell itself could conjure up and drop me into.

He advised me it was being taken in for safe keeping and we would talk about the car when we got to the station. As we drove away from what had been my home, I noticed how much everything had changed. Whole neighborhoods were gone and replaced with large complexes or apartment buildings. The city was nothing like I had remembered. It was then I became scared.

Twenty minutes ago, I had pulled into my driveway and found my time base had moved thirty years. Everything I knew was gone, and in its place was a whole new world. How can this happen in such a short time? Short to me that is.

We arrived at city hall, and yes it was totally different from the city hall I had known. I was placed in an interview room and I remained there for the next hour. One of the officers brought me a cup of coffee and left again without saying a word.

Maybe forty-five minutes later the door opened and a man and woman, both in suits, entered and sat down. They laid several file folders on the table and looked at me. Then the woman spoke. "Mr. Jacobs my name is

Janet Longmeyer and this is Carl Stevens. Mr. Jacobs, we are going to be asking you a number of questions. We know you probably have a few of your own questions you would like to ask, but we are asking you to wait on those questions while we collect some much-needed information.

"After we will try to explain to you what we know and also answer your questions.

Mr. Jacobs, can you tell us what you did today from the time you got up until the police officers contacted you? Please be as detailed as you can, leave nothing out."

I sat there looking at the two of them. The expressions on their faces told me something serious was taking place and I decided to cooperate and answer their questions. "I don't know just where to start, but I guess I could start at the time I got up. I got up at six this morning and took my regular shower. Everything seemed normal. I took fifteen minutes in the shower, got out, shaved and brushed my teeth.

"I got dressed and went out into the kitchen. Helen, my wife, was making my breakfast. Wait what happened to my wife?"

"Mr. Jacobs, we need to have you continue. We'll address that issue shortly. Please continue. I know this is difficult but you must continue."

I knew something really bad was about to land on me but I continued. "The day was clear and it was going to be warm. We had little planned for the day other than me taking a package for my sister to the post office and sending it out. There was no hurry so I decided to do it right after lunch.

"After breakfast Helen asked if I could take the package right then. She wanted to be sure it got out to my sister in the next shipment. So, I agreed and got ready to run to the post office.

"It was no big deal and so I decided to leave the lawn mowing till after lunch. Right after breakfast I got in the car and headed for the post office. That took me around thirty minutes to go there, mail the package and two other letters she had added, and head for home. As I returned home, I noticed things started to look strange."

"Mr. Jacobs what do you mean by strange, and exactly where did you notice this change take place?"

"Well, by strange I mean some of the houses in the neighborhood appeared to be changed or different. I remember stopping at the four way stop at the end of our street and then driving through it and seeing the changes in the houses. It was one of those things a person will note and really think nothing of it. It was when I got home and pulled into the drive way when things started to register.

"It was not that anything was radically changed. The house looked the same but the flower beds were different. Something was not registering. As I got out of the car and walked up to the door, I saw a woman in the kitchen and it wasn't Helen. I tried to open the door and it was locked. The woman came around the corner of the kitchen wall and looked at me and yelled for me to go away. I guess she then went and called the police.

"Five minutes later the police arrived and they told me my license was expired some twenty-nine years earlier. I guess I passed out. Please, what's going on here? What has happened to me?"

Finally, the lady leaned back. "Mr. Jacobs, we don't know what is going on or what has happened. In this folder here we have a report made some thirty years ago. It is a report filed by your wife that you had come up missing. The authorities at the time never found you or your car. Basically, there was no trace of either you or the car and that is the way the report has remained until today.

"In the last six hours wc have gone over your car. That car was almost new thirty years ago. Today when we looked at it there were only three hundred eighty-six miles registered on the odometer. Everything in the car is pristine. All the paper work in the car is dated prior to this day thirty years ago.

"Mr. Jacobs, at the time you were thirty-nine years old. Here is a photograph of you, your wife gave the agency back then. The photograph was six months old when the report was made. Mr. Jacobs, when we compare this photo to you, we can see you have not aged a day in these last thirty years.

"Now sir, that tells us one of two things, you're either not Mr. Jacobs but a very good look alike or something miraculous has happened and you are Mr. Jacobs and in thirty years you have not aged. That includes your car which is absolutely perfect and it leads us to believe you are the original Mr. Jacobs who was reported missing thirty years ago. The real question in this whole unbelievable situation is where have you been these past thirty years?"

All I could do was sit there and look at her. I heard everything she had said but it made no sense. How the hell could a person leave his home to run an errand and then when he returns its thirty years later? Besides I don't feel like I was thirty years older and based on the photo they had of me I had not aged during those thirty years.

This was crazy. There had to be some explanation as to what was going on. It had to be a joke, a rather elaborate one, but a joke none-the-less. I wanted to say something. No, I needed to say something but nothing was coming out. I felt my face flush and I became light headed and started to fall over. The man detective reached out and grabbed me and held me up till I came back.

Finally, it came bursting out of me like a dam had broken. "What is going on here? Please, you need to be honest with me. I don't understand what is happening to me. Where is Helen? Where is my wife? God, this isn't happening to me. Please, please help me?"

Ms. Longmeyer moved her chair around beside me and placed her hands on mine. I turned, looking her in the face. "Mr.

Jacobs, your wife died three years ago. She had been living in an apartment for the past twenty years after giving up on you ever returning. She developed cancer five years ago and finally succumbed to it three years ago. I'm so sorry I had to tell you this, but I think you need the truth right now even if it does hurt."

Helen dead, we would have been married forty-nine years if it is actually 2045. "No, this is crazy. This has to be a test or some kind or a mean joke. You people can't be serious about this. There is no way I could have been gone thirty years and have not known anything about it."

The room fell quiet as we sat there. I guess the other two couldn't think of anything to say and I surely was at a point where I didn't know what to say or if I did, I didn't know how to say it. It was then another officer knocked on the door and stepped in.

He looked at me and then at Detective Longmeyer. "Detective they're here."

She, Detective Longmeyer, looked at me and stood up. "Mr. Jacobs, your children are here and are waiting out in the lobby. Before we take you to meet them you must understand your children have aged these past thirty years. You sir were thirty-nine years old when you disappeared. At the time your oldest son was eighteen then and is now forty-eight. Expect the same changes for your two daughters. Do you understand?"

I started to stand up while looking Detective Longmeyer in the eyes. "No, that can't be? You don't know what you're talking about."

By then I was shaking all over and could hardly stand. Things were piling up on me one on top of the other and it was turning into an avalanche. It then came to me; I didn't want to see anyone. I couldn't take the impact of what that meeting would result in. I sat back down and started to shake my head.

Longmeyer reached over and put her hand on my shoulder. "Mr. Jacobs, you're going to have to see them sooner or later. I really think you need to take this on right now. They have been looking for you for thirty years and now they have the chance of seeing that search come to an end."

I was shaking my head and still trying to deal with the reality I had been thrust into. "But what will they say when they see me. If I was thirty-nine when I disappeared and my son's now forty-eight that will mean I'm the younger and he's my senior. God, that will kill him if not both of us, I just don't know if I'm ready for this."

Longmeyer continued. "I know Mr. Jacobs, but you're just delaying what has to happen sooner or later and besides they want this thing to end. They need closure and they have waited thirty years for it."

I realized she was right and then nodded my head. "You're right, but it's still going to be the hardest thing I have ever done. I just don't know what to expect and how they're going to react."

She put her arm around my shoulder. "Mr. Jacobs, I'll stay with you during the meeting, and if you need anything all you have to do is ask and I'll see you get it."

I stood up and walked around the table as the other detective opened the interview room door and we walked out into a long hallway. "Miss. Longmeyer, I think its best I face them alone. Is that alright with you?"

As we continued to walk down the hallway, she put her hand on my back. "Mr. Jacobs its fine with me, your family will be waiting in a waiting lounge room just off the main entrance. That room has been closed to anyone else using it so you can remain there with your family for as long as you need."

She walked me to the waiting room door and left me standing there. Inside the room were my children I evidently had not seen in thirty years. What was I to say? What would they say? Did I owe them an apology? For a moment I wanted to turn and run, but knew I needed to take the next step and address this thing that has taken over our lives.

CHAPTER TWO

The Meeting

I reached out and took hold of the door knob and turned it. Slowly and easily, I pushed the door open and stepped through. There sitting at the table in the center of the room were three people, one man and two women. All three stood as I entered the room.

We stood there looking at one another waiting for someone to say something or make the first move. The moment was heavy and I could tell all three of them were finding it hard to believe this was happening.

Finally, the man came around the table and walked up to me and put his arms around me. We stood there holding one another, not saying a word. After what seemed like an hour he stepped back. "Dad I'm Patrick."

The name hit me like a hammer. No, this wasn't Patrick, the last time I talked to him was thirty years ago and he was eighteen. I stood there looking at him. "Patrick?"

He was nodding his head. "Yes, dad it's me, Patrick. I was eighteen when you disappeared. At the time we thought you had just up and ran off, but after talking to the detectives and learning about your car and the papers you were carrying, we're trying to come to terms with this whole thing.

"Dad, don't you remember anything about what happened to you and where you were?"

This was moving just too damn fast. My head was spinning as I looked over at the two girls. They must be Jane and Lisa but they are so much older now. Jane was fifteen back then and Lisa was just twelve, now all three are older than I am. "I don't know what to say. Seven hours ago, I was going home from the post office and then here I am, thirty years later. How can this be? How could I have advanced thirty years in time and not remember it? God, it feels like a nightmare."

Both women came around the table and put their arms around me. Jane started to sob. "Dad we were at a loss as to why you had left us and mom like that. Now we're completely at a loss for words or for an understanding as to what has happened."

Lisa was looking at me and trying to say something, finally she got it out. "Dad, you look the same as you did the last time, I saw you thirty years ago. I don't understand what has happened. We missed you so much and now I'm not sure just how I should respond. I don't know where to go from here."

We all stood there looking at one another and after a few moments of indecision I suggested we all sit down. As we took our seats, I placed my elbows on the table top and leaned forward looking at each one individually.

What the hell does one say in a situation like this? The level of stress and confusion was clearly evident in all of us. "I don't know what has happened, and right now I find it hard to believe I am actually awake and sitting here with you. I have been praying this whole thing was a nightmare and I would wake up any time now.

"Somehow I became lost or I was taken or I fell into a hole someplace and just now came out of it. The past thirty years are a total blank. To me, it was only minutes from the time I left the house to go to the post office until I got back and my world had changed. That day, today, when I left the house was the last time, I remember Helen and now I'm told she has passed away. I've lost the better part of my life with her and I'm finding it hard to cope with.

"Then I walk in here and find my three children have aged and every one of you are now older than me. That's not the way it should be. I should be the one who has aged, but I haven't. The truth of the matter is I'm scared half to death and I am even more scared this nightmare is going to continue and not go away."

I felt myself starting to cry. I couldn't help it, the tears just started to run and then I let it all go. The three of them moved in around me and then all the sorrow and pain over these past thirty years came out. I found myself hugging and kissing each of them and looking them in the eyes, God, what I had missed over these thirty years. I knew we had a long way to go and was not quite sure just how we should progress.

I had no sooner thought of that when the door opened and Detective Longmeyer came in. With her was a stately looking man carrying a briefcase. He set the case down on the table and Detective Longmeyer moved around the table to where my children and I were sitting.

"Mr. Jacobs, this is Doctor Paul Evens. Doctor Evens is a Professor of Psychology and we have brought him in to try and assist you in dealing with this situation. It is felt we need to start some type of debriefing as soon as possible so we can come up with some answers as to what has happened to you. Is that all right with you?"

I looked at the Professor and then at the kids and each one of them was nodding their head yes. I knew this much, I needed help and I could never deal with this thing on my own. "Thank you, Detective, and yes I think we need all the help we can get right now."

The Professor sat down at the table and took a note pad out of his case and started to brief us as to what he would be doing. "Mr. Jacobs, I have seen the information the department has developed on you and I find it rather hard to grasp and understand. I'm sorry, but I think I am going to have to have a briefing session of my own before I can really come to terms with what has appeared to have happened. Do you understand?"

I looked at him and felt a sense this was a man who had just been dropped into a game he knew nothing about and was expected to learn how to play as the game moved along. "I understand Professor, but I'm afraid I don't know much more than you do. I guess it would be best for me to relate that part of what has happened that I remember, and then maybe my children can cover the family's side of this for you. Is that all right?"

He was nodding his head. "That will work just fine. Now Mr. Jacobs, please fill me in on everything you remember concerning your activities on the day in question."

I sat back, still holding my daughter's hands. "The best I have been able to figure out it was Saturday June 6th 2015. When I got up that morning it was a beautiful day and Helen was busy making breakfast, it was around seven o'clock.

"We ate our breakfast and then started to talk about what we had planned for the day. She reminded me I had to send a package off that morning and it would be best I did it right away and get it over with. I agreed and got up and went in to the bathroom and shaved and brushed my teeth and finished getting dressed.

"Wait that may not be right, no I think I had done all the personal things first and then went out and had breakfast with Helen.

"I remember getting my keys and wallet and picking up the package and walking toward the back door, stopping on the way and giving Helen a kiss. At that time, she gave me two letters she wanted mailed as well.

"Now I remember, I asked where the kids were and she said both girls had gone to the library with their aunt, they were going to stop and have breakfast first. Patrick was off to football practice and he would be back that afternoon.

"I went out to the garage and got in the car and headed out for the post office. There was nothing unusual, it was just a fine summer day and I was running a simple errand like I had done I don't know how many times in the past.

"I got to the post office and when I entered the main entrance there was a line of people at the mailing desk and so I stepped into line. It took me about twenty minutes to get to the counter and get the package and letters mailed. If I remember right it cost me $4.75 in postage for the package.

"I left the post office building and walked out to the car, unlocked the door and got in. Still nothing odd or different had happened or was happening. I drove home taking the same route back I had driven going to the post office.

"When I turned on to my street, I still did not notice anything unusual until I got to the intersection just before entering the block our house was on. It was then I noticed a change in the houses. By that I mean several of the houses were a different color. Next, I noticed one or two of the houses that had been there when I left were now gone and larger houses were sitting on the lots those houses had been on.

"I was immediately thrown into a state of confusion. I couldn't figure out what was going on. Houses just don't change that fast. I had only been gone maybe thirty to forty-five minutes and the whole of my block had changed. I don't know how long it took me to drive down to the end of the street where our house was. I was trying to cope with or understand what was happening."

I stopped, realizing my recall had changed from the first time I had covered my action with the detectives. I had not said anything about the houses changing other than the flower beds at my house and I had said nothing about the kids.

"I just now realized I had not remembered the changes in the houses until just now. When I first told the detectives about what I remembered I only mentioned the flower beds at my home having changed. Now I remember the other changes as well.

"I thought maybe I got onto the wrong block and was just confused, but several of the houses I recognized as being houses that were on my block. As I approached my house, it was the same house I had left. Except, there were some changes, not to the house, but to the flower beds in front of the house. The flower beds were bigger and stuck out into the yard much further than they did an hour ago.

"As I pulled into the driveway, I had this feeling come over me things were not right. I sat there looking the house over and decided it had been painted sometime in the not-too-distant past and they had used the same paint color. There were other things that didn't look right. I knew it was my house, but still something told me it was not.

"Again, I'm remembering additional actions I had not covered before. I can't figure this out, but I need to keep going."

Just then Detective Longmeyer came into the room with a tray full of cups and a pot of coffee. "Pardon me, but I thought maybe someone would like some coffee."

I nodded and she poured a cup and handed it to me. The others, including the Professor, acknowledged they wanted one as well. When she finished, she left the pot and left the room.

Professor Evens set his cup down. "Please Mr. Jacobs will you continue with your briefing?"

"Yes, let's see I was or had just pulled into my driveway and I was looking at the house. I now remember the changes to the house and had not covered those before. I guess my memory is improving

"I got out and walked up to the back door and it was locked. I tried my key and it would not work so I knocked on the door. Oh, as I approached the back door, I saw a woman in the kitchen and it wasn't Helen. When I knocked on the door, she looked around the wall from the kitchen and told me to go away. I tried to tell her this was my house and I guess that was when she called the police.

"By the time they got there I was sitting on the steps trying to understand what was going on. There was this strange woman in my house telling me to go way and now the police were walking up to me. They asked for my identification and I handed it to them.

"As the officer looked at my driver's license, he kept looking at me and then back to the license. That's when he asked me if I knew my license had expired. I told him I did not and he then told me it had expired twenty-nine years ago. That was the first time, the first second I knew something unbelievable was going on.

"I mean, how I, in less than an hour, could lose twenty-nine or thirty years in time. That was crazy, no it was insane crazy. I didn't believe him and it was then they took me into custody. Once they started checking my car and then checking my name in their records, they learned I had gone missing thirty years earlier.

"So here I am as you see me. I have three children all older than I am. My wife died sometime in the past and the house I thought was mine is no longer mine. Professor, what else could happen to me that could be any worse than what I have just related to you?"

He sat there looking at his notes. I knew he was having one hell of a time dealing with what was obvious to him and everyone else. What I had just laid on him was something no one had ever been faced with in all time. It was impossible, but here it was, a man sitting there in front of him who had disappeared thirty years earlier and was now back and had not changed one bit from the moment when he disappeared. Even his car was the same as it had been that day those thirty years ago. Clearly there was no room for a false claim here, it was the real thing.

He finally looked up and shrugged his shoulders. "Mr. Jacobs, I'm at a loss as to what to say or where to go from here. Obviously, this is all true because I have looked at your car, and I have seen the police reports from thirty years ago, and now I find you here today. In case you didn't know it, they have already compared your fingerprints from then to now and it's all a match.

"Mr. Jacobs, thirty years ago you went somewhere, someplace and you have now returned and we have not the slightest idea as to where you have been or what has happened to you. This situation is well beyond any psychological issue and I feel we will need to bring in scientists from several different fields in order to fully address this. My problem sir, is whether that is what you want to do?"

What I wanted to do, hell I didn't even know where I wanted to go. I needed something and I needed it now. No, I couldn't go on without finding out where I had been. I finally sat back and looked the Professor in the eyes. "Sir, I will not continue on without knowing where I have been. There is just no way I can handle my life from here on out without knowing where the past thirty years went. Whatever it takes I want to know, no I need to know where I have been."

The Professor sat there looking at me and then my children. He finally shrugged his shoulders. "Mr. Jacobs, I'm not sure if we can do that. So far everything we have been able to figure out in this case tells us you have in fact been away for those thirty years. You, your clothes, your papers, your car all tell us you are back here in exactly the same way you were when you dropped out of sight those many years ago.

35

"I have a feeling we are going to have to do some real deep research on your situation before we can even make a guess as to what happened. This much I will tell you, if you're willing to help, we are going to try and work this thing out."

I was sitting there looking at a man completely at a loss as to what he should or could do. "Professor, I can only tell you whatever is decided at this time, I am in support of it completely. I want to know what has happened and why it has happened. Professor, I need to know everything. I cannot live with this thing, anything still unanswered. Something terrible happened to me thirty years ago and now I'm in a situation where I need answers, and I would like to have them as soon as possible."

Finally, he stood up and started to collect the papers he had placed on the table top and looked right at me. "Mr. Jacobs, I am going to leave you with your children for the time being. Please understand I have a lot of preparation to do before we can get started. If it is alright with you, I will get to work on those preparations and then contact you in a week.

"At that time, I will want you to come to our facility and plan on staying there for however long it takes us to come up with an answer. I must tell you I have no idea right now as to how or what we are going to start with, but I can tell you we are going to do something. Is that agreeable with you?"

What else could I do? My problem now was determining where I was going to go. I looked at my children and felt so uneasy. Not one of the three had said a word since the professor had come into the room. They were just sitting there watching me and what they were thinking I could only imagine. Finally, I formulated the questions. "What do you three thinks of this?"

My son looked at me and placed his elbows on the table top. "Sir, I don't know what to say. I guess you could come home with me but you need to understand I'm not sure how to respond to you. Yes, you're my father, but I'm older than you. That is not settling well with me and I really don't know just how things would work out if you came to live with me and my family."

I knew then I wasn't their father, I was an oddity and they had no idea how to treat me. All I could do was sit there looking at them. I wasn't their father; he was dead and buried thirty years ago. I was something from the past maybe they preferred not to deal with.

I couldn't help it, the tears started to run as I sat there looking at them. What the hell could I say anyway? They had lived the better part of their lives without a father and they had no idea what had happened to me or why I had left them. I couldn't blame them; they were just kids then and one day I left the house and thirty years later I came back.

Just then Lisa got up and walked around the table and sat down beside me and put her arms around my shoulders. I laid my head on her shoulder and cried. It wasn't long before she was crying as well and then I felt the hands of the other two on my back, being held by all three.

That went on for the next five minutes or so and during that time the professor stood there watching this most difficult moment in all our lives.

Finally, Lisa looked me in the eyes. "Dad, I don't know what happened back then or what is happening here right now, but I know you are my father and until this mess is cleared up, I want you to come to my home and stay with me.

"I have no family and maybe between the two of us we can start this process of figuring out just what happened to you back then. Dad, we all need to know just as much as you do. There is a huge empty hole in our lives and we have to know why and what caused it."

I was nodding my head and looking at the three of them. It came to me I had to say something, so I took a deep breath. "I want the three of you to know I did not leave you or Helen. Please, I have no idea what has happened or where I went. That day was just a normal day and then everything changed. One second, I was there in 2015 and the next second I'm here in 2045.

"I'm scared and hurt. I've lost everything I valued and left Helen to deal with it all, and I will never be able to live it down. If we can't figure this thing out then I would rather be dead. I have to know what happened, and you deserve to know as well. I want you to know here and now nothing is outside being discussed or asked. You have questions and I may or may not be able to answer them, but I'll try and if I can't then we will find the answer between the four of us."

We finally all stood up and walked out of the room to the main entrance. The Professor shook my hand and advised he would call me by the end of the week and set up the schedule.

Detective Longmeyer walked up to us and advised she had all she needed and I could go with my children. She would keep in touch with us during the follow up investigation of my situation and if I needed anything, I could call her at any time.

As I turned to walk out the front entrance of the station, I had a thought and turned back to the Detective. "Ms. Longmeyer."

"Yes, Mr. Jacob."

"Ms. Longmeyer, what is going to happen to my car?"

She walked up to me. "Mr. Jacobs, we will hold your car here at the station for the time being. It has been placed in a secure garage and will be held there until we have some answers. In time it will be returned to you, but not right now."

I understood the necessity of maintaining the facts of my case and nodded my head. "Thank you, Ms. Longmeyer, you have been helpful and supportive of me all during this mess. I'll not worry about the car until later."

With that we turned and walked out the door and into this new life I had been thrust into.

CHAPTER THREE

Dreams and Feelings

Almost an hour later we were pulling into the driveway of Lisa's home. It was a small cottage type home, well-kept and maintained. As we walked up to the front door it dawned on me, I didn't have any clothes or necessities. All I had was what I was wearing.

Apparently, the same thought hit her at the same time. She looked at me. "We'll go downtown later and get you some clothes and necessities. Right now, I think you need a meal and a chance to relax for a few minutes."

I nodded my head as she opened the door and we walked into the house. Almost immediately I noticed the painting on the wall over her couch. It was the same one that had been in our living room back home. Helen had selected that painting two days after we bought our home, we had been married five years at the time.

As I looked over the room Lisa went into the kitchen and started to fix us something to eat. She called out. "Is there anything in particular you would like to have?"

Then it hit me, I had only had breakfast a few hours ago and just coffee for lunch. No wait, I had my last breakfast thirty years ago and the coffee just a few hours ago. Odd, but that's the way it felt. "No, just anything that is convenient."

It was then I saw a picture on the end table. I walked over and picked it up and looked at the four faces in the photo. It was of Helen and the three kids. The sorrow washed over me as I stood there looking down at the four of them. I realized I was a victim, but they were victims as well. This whole mess was no one's fault and we all had lost so much.

Just then Lisa called me into the kitchen. She had set a cup of hot soup on the table alongside a sandwich. I sat down as she sat down on the other side of the table. I took a drink of the soup and then a bite of the sandwich. As I started to chew the sandwich, I bit my tongue and almost choked on the sandwich. I leaned over the table and spit the sandwich parts out of my mouth along with a considerable amount of blood.

Lisa jumped up and moved around to me with a towel and started wiping my lips off and trying to help me recover from the chocking. "Dad what's going on?"

I finally recovered enough to answer her. "I forgot how to chew. I forgot how to eat."

I have never been so scared in all my life. I could not eat, well not right then. I would have to learn how to do that all over again.

She removed the sandwich from the table and then when to the refrigerator and brought back a bowl of pudding and placed it in front of me. "Now start by eating this. Take your time, don't push it."

I looked up at her. "Lisa, I don't think I have eaten anything in thirty years. I don't know how I know that, but I know in that period of time I had not eaten anything."

She immediately went into the living room and a couple of minutes later came back with a writing pad and pen. She sat down and started to write down everything that had just happened and what I had said. She then looked at me. "Now we are going to record everything you say and do from here on out. If you see or feel anything that does not seem right then you need to tell me and we'll record it."

I was nodding my head and I started to eat the pudding. The taste hit me strange. It was good but seemed to be quite strong. I think it was chocolate. I continued to eat and take my time to make sure I did everything right. I looked over at her. "This is odd. I know I ate this morning and it was just fine, but right now I'm having a difficult time doing it. Something as simple as eating is a problem for me. Why is that?"

She was writing down all I was saying and then replied. "Well dad it could be you did not eat for the thirty-year period. I don't know how that could be, but the only way you could forget how to eat is by not eating for a long time."

I then realized every experience I would have while re-accustoming to being home would be a new experience. Now my mind was starting to function and starting to

45

address all that had happened to me over these past thirty years. I had a feeling I may not what to re-live it, but I also knew I had to if I was ever going to get this figured out.

After lunch Lisa took me to town and we bought some clothes and necessities and returned to her home. The shopping was an experience in that the changes in the styles of clothes, the design of the stores and the many kinds of products were almost beyond my understanding. Everything had changed and I was going to find it most difficult learning everything all over again.

We spent the rest of the afternoon talking about what had happened to the kids during those thirty years. I looked at Lisa. "When did Mom get sick?"

I guess she had been expecting that question. "Dad, she was diagnosed with a cancerous tumor in her brain five years before she died.

"We did chemo and radiation but nothing seemed to slow it down. She kept saying she would try to last for as long as possible in case you came home. She wanted to see you one last time."

The realization of what she had gone through was starting to set in. Along with that,

I could feel the anger building in me. To know what she went through and she was still waiting for my return made me want to strike out at anyone or anything. Damn, this was getting out of control.

That night as I settled down to sleep, I felt a tinge of tightness settle over my body. I rolled over on my side and tried to go to sleep. My mind was running through all that had happened since I got up that morning, thirty years ago. How and why, kept running across my mind. I started to think about Helen and all she had gone through. I don't remember going to sleep.

I don't know how long I had slept when I had this feeling something was watching me. I tried to roll over and face the opposite direction but the same feeling was there.

I finally rolled onto my back and opened my eyes. The room was dark but there was something else. No, that's not it, there was nothing else. I felt for the bed and there was nothing there. Wait, now I'm dreaming this, there had to be something there. I was prone and, on my back, and I felt like I was laying on something. But there was nothing there. Yes, I was prone but I was floating in free space with nothing under me or around me.

Fear charged through my body as I came to grips with the fact I was not in my daughter's bedroom and the bed was gone as well. I was someplace, but no place. It then came to me I was all alone, completely and totally alone.

No wait there was something there, something was watching me. I couldn't hear or see anything; it was just a feeling that it was there. It was moving around me and watching my reactions.

The next thing that touched me was that I had been here before and that feeling of another's presence I had known before. What the hell was going on? I knew it wanted to know what I was feeling and how I was coping with this situation. I felt like a lab rat unable to do anything to change the situation I found myself in.

Finally, I found my voice and yelled out. "Where am I? What am I doing here?"

There was silence, just that continuous sense something was watching, measuring, indulging in my circumstance. Then I heard it. "You know where you're at."

"What? What did you say?"

48

It came back. "You know where you're at."

It wasn't a question it was a statement of fact. I was supposed to know where I was. It expected me to know and I had a feeling thing would remain as they currently were until I remembered. "No please, I don't understand. What is this? What is going on?"

"Open you mind and think. You know where you're at. Stop trying to deny it and accept the fact." The voice or message sounded more forceful, more demanding and more impatient.

Next thing I know I'm screaming and trying to get up and reach out and grab whatever it was that was tormenting me. Just then I felt something grab me and then I heard her voice. "Dad, wake up. Dad, you're having a nightmare."

Next thing I know I'm looking at Lisa and she is talking to me in a quiet and controlled voice. "Dad, you're in your bed and you have been dreaming. Do you understand me? You're in your bed and everything is all right."

I felt me shaking my head and reaching up and grabbing her arms just above the elbow. "No, it's trying to make me remember where I have been. It's trying to get me to come back to it or something like that. It's alive and it's still after me."

This was crazy. I knew I had experienced something real and not a dream yet I couldn't prove it. I knew then and there I needed to pursue this somehow and come up with what happened to me thirty years ago.

I knew this much. That may have been a dream, but the feeling I had while experiencing it was real. I felt it clear down into my soul and it was real. Something, some being, was still connected to me and I knew if I didn't do something soon it was going to reclaim me.

That raised the question. Have I come back from some process or event that had been ended by some benevolent being's concern for me? I may have come back by means of escape and if so, then why don't I remember it?

I finally calmed down. Lisa sat down on the bed by me. "Can you tell me what you saw or heard in that nightmare?"

I looked at her and realized she was really scared but was controlling herself. "I don't know. It seems to me it started with my realizing I was in a dark void and the bed was gone and there was nothing around me but blackness.

"I could feel something there, not an object but a living or existing being or something. I could tell it was watching me intently and then I felt myself start to scream.

"It was then that it started to communicate with me. I don't know if it was speaking out loud or if it was just in my mind, but it said to me. "You know where you're at."

"It kept saying that and then told me, open your mind and you'll know where you're at." That's all I remember but I'm telling you it was real and besides I now think I know what it was. I don't know how or what this is all about, but deep inside I know what that thing is or was. God help me but I know, I just can't say it or bring it to the front of my mind.

"Besides, if and when I do, I'm afraid I'll go crazy or better yet I'll die. Lisa, I need help and you're not the one who can give it to me. If you try, I feel you'll become a target of this thing, whatever it is, and that could mean your death."

I was looking around the bedroom by this time and trying to determine if anything physical had been left or remained of this encounter. There was nothing there, but I had this deep down feeling the link was still there and it, whatever it was, was just on the other side and waiting.

"All right Dad, we'll leave things as they are right now and then contact the professor in the morning is that all right?"

I was nodding my head. "Yeah, that will help but I'm not going to be able to sleep anymore tonight. In fact, I can't stay here in this bedroom. If it's all right with you I'll get up and go in to the living room and sit there until morning?"

She nodded her head. "Do you want me to stay up with you?"

"No, you go to bed, I don't think there will be any more trouble tonight as long as I'm awake. I just can't sleep right now and I need to do some thinking on this whole mess."

With that I got up and put on my robe and went out to the kitchen and started to put on a pot of coffee. She followed me and then sat down at the table. I looked at her and I could see the question building in her face. "What is it Lisa, what do you want to ask me?"

She looked down at the table top and them back up to me. "Dad, I have listened to everyone talking during the past day and I have heard every kind of thought as to what happened to you. But still, I can't get it out of my mind you left us and Mom at a time when it was most important in our lives.

"That hurt has been there all these years and all three of us have tried to deal with it in our own way. But now you're back and there is a mountain of questions as to where you went and why you came back now. I don't understand any of this, whatever it is that is happening.

My heart has been so full of hurt and anger toward you. The others feel the same way that's why they hesitated accepting you in their homes when it came time to leave the police station.

"Dad, we all thought you had just run off to some place and would never come back. Then you show up in the way you did. It was beyond belief, yet there it is. Dad, we just don't know how to handle this. Damn it anyway, it would have been better if you hadn't come back."

She sat there with tears running down her face. I couldn't be mad at her; she was being honest and I could tell what she was saying was true. They must have thought the worst of me and I don't blame them. My problem now is to get them to understand I did not do this of my own will but something had taken me.

How the hell did I know? Something had taken me? But to where? Why all these years, and for what reason? She needed an answer and I needed one as well. What was I to say to her anyway?

Finally, I walked over to the table and sat down across from her. "Lisa, I understand what you're saying and it hurts, when I realize what Helen and you kids went through. I don't have an answer for you as to why and where I went because I don't know. Lisa, I don't understand this thing anymore than you kids. One minute I'm headed home from the post office and the next I'm pulling into my driveway thirty years later."

I could feel the tears running down my face and dropping off my chin onto the table top. "To tell you the truth, I would just as soon be dead than to be here under these circumstances. I hate this, whatever happened ruined my life, the lives of my wife and children and it destroyed the future we could have lived together. But I can tell you this, it's not over yet. Do you understand me? Whatever has happened is not over yet and I fear things are about to get worse."

She got up and moved around the table and pulled me around and sat down in my lap. She put her arms around my neck and buried her face in my shoulder and just sat there holding me. I felt myself reach up and wrap my arms around her and then pull her closer to me.

After several minutes she sat up straight and looked me in the eyes. "Dad, we are going to work our way through this. Whatever has happened, we are going to find out what it was and then we are going to deal with it. If there is some being involved in this thing, then we will need to deal with that as well. What is important is we are together again and we are going to work through this and stay together."

I could see she was serious. It was then I realized her determination and the look on her face was Helen through and through. I reached out and took her hand. "Lisa, I agree with you and that means I'm going to have to sit down and try to remember all I can about my life and everything that has happened to me since 2015."

She stood up and turned to me. "Dad, that would help a lot, but right now I need to get back to bed. Its three thirty and I need to be up at seven so I can get to work on time. Is that all right with you?"

I nodded and she bent over and kissed me on the cheek and left me sitting there to think about my past. I got up and got a writing pad and pen from her kitchen desk and returned to the table, after getting another cup of coffee. I then began to write.

The first thing to entered my mind was the day I left or was taken. I sat back and let my mind go back to that day to try and bring out the details up to and including the moment I left. I thought it was going to be difficult and then I remembered it happened yesterday and I should be able to bring it all back.

I remember Helen had gotten up at her usual, around six in the morning. I usually stay in bed till eight or so. It was a fine day, just like yesterday, and I was looking forward to it. I was actually up at seven and took a shower.

There was nothing unusual that morning. I felt great and the shower was most relaxing. Thirty minutes later I was finished and walking into the kitchen to fix myself something to eat. Normally I have an egg with toast and a cup of coffee and then I'm ready for the day.

Yesterday, I remember going out and getting the paper and Helen placing my breakfast on the table, and sitting down at the table to eat and read the news. Helen had gone into the living room to work on a few letters she said she needed to get out that day.

I had finished breakfast and had just put the dishes in the dishwasher when Helen came into the kitchen with a couple of letters and a small package. "Dear, would you run to the post office and send these things out for me this morning?"

I took the letters and package from her and noted the package was to my sister. "Yeah, I can do that right now, and then I have to get home and get started on mowing the lawn."

She smiled at me and gave me a kiss. "You look refreshed this morning did you have a good night's sleep?"

"Yes, as a matter of fact I did."

Details, it was the details I needed to work on. Right now, things were a little haphazard. I was getting the sequence of events mixed up as I retold that day's events each time. Just now I had the breakfast thing mixed up but knew the description I had just written down was correct when I compare it to the prior descriptions. I knew my mind needed to work on getting everything straight and clear and it was going to be a process I needed to work through.

I continued: We then talked about a few things around the house she would like to see done that day. At the same time, I was getting my wallet and keys and heading for the door to make the run to the post office. She walked with me to the back door and then gave me a kiss to send me on my way.

All right now I remember we talked about a number of things and she walked with me to the back door. That was clearly new information and again I knew it was right.

I remember backing out of the driveway. Ralph the neighbor to our west was already out mowing his lawn and he looked over and gave me a wave. I waved back and put the car in gear and pulled away.

Our neighborhood is a quiet and well-kept neighborhood. Our home is located almost dead center on the block. The name of our street is Monroe Street. Each house sits on a sixty-five by one hundred fifty-foot lot. There are sidewalks and curbs running parallel to the street. Most homes have at least one tree in the parking strip in front of the house. You know what I mean, a simple but typical suburban neighborhood.

What was going on here? My mind seemed to be opening up and the amount of detail was expanding with each moment. I had to keep going and keep the memories coming. I knew it would all be important later on.

As you drive east on Monroe you first come to 4th Avenue, there is a four way stop sign at Monroe and 4th. I continued through and to the next main street and on to the post office. There was nothing, absolutely nothing that stood out as being unusual during my trip to the post office.

It took me maybe twenty minutes mailing the package and letters and then I returned to my car. I noted I usually see someone I knew while there but had seen no one that day. I left the parking lot and headed home taking the same route I took to get there.

Again, everything was the same as I headed home. I don't remember anything being odd or out of the ordinary during this time. I turned onto Monroe Street and headed for the house. As I approached 4th, I started to slow for the stop sign and it was then I started to remember something.

As I think about it, I thought there was something odd going on. It was like I was looking through crystal clear water. Everything around me looked normal and everything in front of me looked like I was looking through water. I stopped for the stop sign and then pulled ahead and passed into the water view. I remember a black spot as I passed through. It was only a second in time, but it was definitely a black spot.

How can I explain that experience? It was like cutting a piece of wood and then looking at the grain layout of the cut. That cross section told me the number of layers that were in the wood and the density and color of each layer. It was the same as I moved or started through the intersection.

There was the water layer that felt like it was as thick as the car was long. Then a dark zone, actually it was black, as black as can be and it too seemed to be thick like the length of the car. Then another water effect, it too was the same thickness.

That water effect I find interesting and hard to describe. I call it water because it makes me think of when you look through a glass of clear water and how it distorts everything on the other side. All I know is there was some medium there the dark or black was sandwiched between, the two water effects.

It came to me this was in itself odd in that, if there was a black section there why then could I see all the way through the two water view sections. That part I had no answer for, unless the black was the actual thirty-year jump in time I had experienced.

After passing through the visual effect, it was then I noticed the changes on Monroe Street. That was it, I had passed through some kind of a gate, some kind of a door or something and after that point I was looking at my street, Monroe Street thirty-years later. I had no sense of time passing or lost. It was just the visual effect and that second of blackness that I recall.

I looked down at my wrist watch and noted it was running but the date was still 2015. The time was correct but the date was off by thirty-years. I then took the watch off and laid it on the table. As I removed my hand the minute and hour hands of the watch started to move. As I watched it, they moved faster and faster. At the same time the date started to change, advancing one day at a time toward the current time.

I sat there for an hour watching my watch move through time. It finally registered today's date, 2045 and stopped. It had caught up with time and was now synchronized with today's time and date. It was a stunning effect and left me almost breathless. It had actually been showing my originating time in 2015 and then when I removed it from my body it advanced and synchronized itself to 2045.

All I could do was sit there looking at it. What the hell else could I do? This was crazy and I was finding it harder to grasp all that had happened to me. I picked the watch up and as soon as I did it started to run backward in the same manner it had when it was synchronizing to the current time.

I sat there watching it moving in reverse until it hit the right time as now but in the year 2015. When the watch was on me it would go back to the time I went away and when off me it would come back to the current time and date.

What does this all mean anyway? Does it mean I'm still in that time period? What would you call it, a Time Warp? No, it's a Time Trap.

I continued to record all my thoughts and happenings for the next two hours. By the time I set the pen down I had filled the writing pad and was ready to start another. It was then Lisa came into the kitchen and went over to the coffee pot and poured a cup. She turned to me. "How did it go last night?"

I sat there and pushed the writing pad toward her. "I sat down and started to write down everything I could remember about yesterday. As you can see, I got a lot of writing done. Do you have time to sit down and go over what I have recorded?"

She looked at her watch and then nodded. "Sure, what do you want me to look at or do you want me to read the whole thing?"

I sat there and shook my head no. "Lisa, I'm going to show you something that may or may not cause you to have some fearful feelings about this whole situation. What I'm going to show you was something I came across completely by accident, but it's so dramatic I don't want to do anything but show it to you."

She set her cup down and leaned across the table toward me. "All right dad, show me what you have."

I reached over and undid my watch and set it on the table in front of her. At first, she just looked down at it and said nothing or showed no reaction to the watch. You could see what she was seeing slowly crawl across her face. Her eyes got bigger and bigger and she tried to say something several time and each time fell silent again.

She sat there all the time the watch was synchronizing itself to the current time and when it finally stopped, she looked up at me. Her eyes were full of disbelief with the realization she had witnessed something so outlandish there were no words she could say that would competently address the issue. In addition, the watch had only taken twenty minutes this time to synchronize.

"Yes, Lisa that's what you have seen. While on my wrist my watch is keeping my current time, which happens to be in 2015. When I remove it from my wrist it starts to advance and synchronize itself with your current time. Also, when I pick it up it starts

"Once we have met with them, we are going to contact the professor and make arrangements to meet with him today and get this thing moving." She sat there watching me and waiting for my reaction to what she had just said.

It was obvious her experience with my watch had finally cut through all the doubt and suspicion the three of them were living with. Now I felt for the first time I had someone on my side and we could start to get some things done. I still had the fear sitting in my mind as a result of my experience that night, and it would not go away.

She picked up the phone and made a call. "Hi Jane, hey, I have just had something happen over here with dad I think you need to know about. But even more important there is something you need, no you must see. What's a good time for you?"

She stood there listening and then started to nod her head as she looked over at me. "All right, we'll be there at that time. I'm going to try and have Patrick meet us there as well. Jane, this is really important and I cannot tell you or describe to you what has happened over the phone. We'll see you in two hours."

She dialed the phone again and waited for an answer. Finally, the phone on the other end was answered. "Hi Mary, is Patrick there?" There was a pause. "Hi Pat, we need to meet with you. Can you get away say in two hours and meet us over at Jane's place?"

Again, she stood there nodding and then an angry look came over her face. "Pat, you cut that out right now. Something has happened over here and you must see it. When you do you will understand what has happened and I can assure you it will change your attitude."

She was listening intently and then started to nod her head again. "Yes, you can bring Mary. We'll see you in two hours at Jane's place, bye Pat."

She put the phone down and turned to me. "You know what dad, I think I'll call Professor Evans and ask if he can meet with us at Jane's house as well, what do you think?"

All this time I had been sitting there watching Lisa set up this meeting. I could tell her brother and sister listened to her and she was rather forceful. The fact was I could see her mother all through her. I nodded my head. "Yeah, I think you're right about that. We need to get moving on this and start getting people on my side. Lisa, we need to cut through all the distrust, anger and doubt that were clearly evident in the other two."

We had two hours to prepare for the meeting. I got cleaned up and dressed and was back in the kitchen within forty-five minutes. She was at the counter preparing a number of food items to take with us. She looked at me. "It always helps if there is a little food available while dealing with stressful issues."

She smiled and continued in her preparations. Yeah, I could see a lot of Helen in her and realized just how much I was missing Helen. The real pain of losing her had not set in yet, but I knew it was coming. It just seemed there was too much going on and the threat of that thing from last night was still looming in the background. But I knew in time it was coming.

By the time Lisa was done and finished getting herself ready it was time to head out. As we were backing out of the driveway, she looked over at me. "Oh, I got ahold of the professor and invited him and he will be able to make it."

"Good, I was hoping he could make it. I think we're going to be depending on him and his expertise. I'm not sure how he will be able to help, but I feel he will be a major force in this."

We sat there in silence the rest of the way to Jane's. It was just under a thirty-minute drive to her house and as we arrived Patrick was just pulling up as well. I watched as Patrick and his wife walked up to us. She walked right up to me and offered her hand. "Hi dad, I'm Mary."

I took her hand and stood there looking at her. "Mary I'm so happy to meet you I only wish it was under better circumstances and not this mess we find ourselves in."

She nodded her head and let go of my hand and put her arms around me and gave me a tight and lingering hug. It was something I needed.

By the time we had all exited our cars the professor pulled up and parked in the street and approached us. He walked up to me and offered his hand. "David, how are you doing today?"

I took his hand. "Well right now I'm doing great but last night was a nightmare. I think we'll be talking about that shortly."

He nodded and shook Lisa's, Patrick's and Mary's hands and we all walked up to

Jane's front door. As we approached the house, she opened the door and welcomed us all in. I walked up to her and started to reach out and she turned away from me. It was obvious she was not ready or willing to rebuild our father and daughter relationship. I let it pass.

We all went into the living room and were finding our seats as Lisa took the eats into the kitchen and started to set them out. She was looking into the living room. "Give me a couple of minutes and I'll have this stuff all set up and then we can start."

The air was heavy as Jane and Patrick moved over to the couch and sat down together, nether one wanting to look at me or recognize my presence. Mary moved over to a chair in the corner of the living room. The professor was busy getting his notebook out and setting up a recorder.

He looked around the room. "Is there any problem with me recording this meeting? I think it's going to be important we record our reactions and feelings during this meeting.

"If what Lisa has told me is factual, I think the three of us, you Jane, Patrick and I are going to be experiencing something that is going to have a big impact."

As he looked around everyone was nodding in agreement, he nodded and continued to set up the recorder. By this time Lisa had returned to the living room and moved over and sat down beside me. The other two noted the act and appeared to be a little surprised by Lisa's action.

We all sat there for a moment and then Lisa spoke up. "All right, let's get this going. Right now, I think this meeting is for one reason and one reason only, and that is to clear up the issue of dad's disappearance. Jane, Patrick, you have been dealing with this for the last thirty years just as I have and then out of nowhere dad reappears.

"I was just as angry as you were, but in the past twelve hours I have come to learn just what has taken place and now it's time for you to learn the same thing.

"Now listen to me carefully, this is not a joke or a trick. What you are about to experience is factual and it will explain a lot as to what has happened over these past thirty years. All I want you to do is to sit there and observe. Don't say a word, just observe. Do you understand?"

The two of them looked at one another then over to Lisa and they both nodded. Lisa then turned to me. "All right, dad, show them the watch."

I stood up and walked over to the coffee table and took my wrist watch off and laid it on the table. As I did both Jane and Patrick and then the professor leaned forward and looked at the watch.

As I pulled my hand away the watch started in. Both the minute and hour hands started running clockwise and started to pick up speed. The three of them had their eyes glued on the watch as it continued increasing its speed in its march to synchronization with the current time.

I stepped back and sat back down by Lisa and we waited. Jane reached over and took Pat's left hand with both her hands and held on. When the watch had finally synchronized, I noted two things. The synchronization only took fifteen minutes where it had taken a half hour the last time and both Jane and Patrick were in a state of shock.

Up till now the professor had said nothing. I looked over at him and he was sitting there looking at the watch. You could see his mind was going a million miles an hour. Finally, he looked over at me and reached over and picked up the watch and held it out to me. He then asked. "What happens when you put it back on?"

I took the watch and placed it back onto my wrist and the hands started moving again, except this time they moved counter clockwise. "That is how it has been every time I have done this except this time it only involved fifteen minutes. The first time it took an hour for it to complete the synchronization and the second time thirty minutes."

He sat there watching the minute and hour hand spinning around on the watch. He then started to shake his head and looked up at me. "That is the damnedest thing I have ever seen. However, I have a concern."

I looked at him. "What's the matter?"

He was shaking his head. "David, what I have just seen only confirms what you have experienced. The problem is if the watch re-synchronizes every time you take it off and put it back on then that tells me you yourself are still out of sync with our time. David, you're still back at your original time thirty years ago before you went missing.

"David, somehow you have jumped ahead in time. Somehow you have moved from your time in 2015 to our time here in

2045. You have not been gone thirty years; you have only been gone a few hours by your time. What you have found is what the future would have been if you had actually disappeared back then, thirty years ago."

What the hell was he saying anyway? Now I was really mixed up and as I looked at the others you could see the confusion in their faces. "Wait a minute now, what you're saying is I have not been gone thirty years but have only been gone for a few hours? But I'm right here thirty years later, I don't understand?"

He sat back looking at the table top and then looked over at me. "David, I'm not sure I can explain it to you. Something has happened that has driven you thirty years into the future. You are physically here and your children have experienced thirty years of your being gone. To them the time frame is real. However, your time frame is off by thirty years and it's that time frame that has caused the trauma your family has lived through."

I stood up looking at him. "This is nuts. How the hell can that be? I know I'm real and I'm flesh and blood standing here right in front of you. I can reach out and touch each of you and you're flesh and blood as well.

Professor I simply don't understand what you're saying.

"If this is true then I'm even more afraid than I was when this thing first happened."

Lisa reached up and took hold of my hand and pulled me back down. I looked at her and there was a lost look in her eyes. Lisa squeezed my hand and then looked at the professor. "Professor we have been writing everything down dad has been able to remember including his experience last night."

She took the notebooks and handed them to him. He took it and sat back and opened the first one and started to read. As he went over the information there, he kept looking up at me. Finally, he set the last notebook down and leaned forward. "David, the voice you heard last night, can you describe it? I mean can you tell us what it sounded like and whether it was intelligent or just what?"

He had centered on the being from last night and his question seemed to drive itself into my mind. I sat there looking at him and then felt I needed to recall that thing and see if

I could give him the information he was wanting.

"I guess I can do that. "I went to bed and had been asleep for a period of time when I had a feeling there was something or someone in the room with me. When I opened my eyes, it was as black as black can be. I felt like I was floating and I could not feel the bed under me.

"At first I could hardly hear the voice but I knew it was there. I had to strain to hear it and I kept crying out. I remember asking where I was and the voice kept coming back saying I knew where I was.

It was an authoritative voice, a voice that had power and control in it. It never changed its tone, by that I mean it was monotone. The only thing it said to me was that I knew where I was.

"The damn thing was pissing me off and I remember screaming at it and asking who it was and where it was. All it would say was I knew where I was."

I looked over at Patrick and Jane and they were both looking at me like I was a totally different being. Jane got up and walked over to me and knelt down in front of me and laid her head on my legs. I reached up and ran my hand through her hair. If nothing else they now knew this was real and something extremely unreal had happened to me.

Pat sat there looking at me and the professor and then back to me. He finally found his voice. "Dad, now that I've seen this thing happen, I realize I had judged you wrongly. Please forgive me for that. But there is still something going on and I don't know just what we're going to do about it.

"If the professor is right, then you may only be here for a short time and we'll lose you again. I'm confused and scared at the same time but, I know if we can get you back to the moment when you passed through that intersection, then all that has happened in these last thirty years will change for us."

At last, all three were on the same page and now knew this whole mess was something out of their and my control. I looked at them. "Look you three, God, I don't know what I'm saying, I know something is wrong and it has to be corrected, just how we do that I'm not sure. If I go back to the exact moment, will it do what needs to be done to correct this. I don't know if that will do it. What I do know is there is something really strange and scary going on and I still have this being to deal with as well."

I didn't know if I was making any sense in what I was saying, but I continued. "It appears I have been pulled out of my time for a reason. The voice told me I knew what the reason was and I needed to remember. That makes me think I am here for something important, something that will impact you here at this time. Kids, there is a reason I am here and it's not that I have been gone for thirty years. No, it's something that is tied to me and not you.

CHAPTER FIVE

Finding the Key

"Look everyone; I think David's time here is limited." The professor was looking at all of us. "Something had taken place back in 2015 that has placed him here in our time.

"What we need to do now is to figure out what has happened and then see if we can address this whole thing from that perspective." He then turned to me. "Now David, can you tell us what was going on in detail that day in 2015?

"David, I'm not talking about your personal existence I am talking about what was going on around your community, your state, your nation and the world at that time. What kind of work, were you involved in? Do you understand? What worldwide or personal event was in the process at the time?"

I looked at the professor and then at the others. "If there had been something specific going on in the world at that time you would know it just a well as I would. You were all there except you were all thirty years younger."

The professor was shaking his head. "No David, it does not work that way. Your being here thirty years later after the family assumed you had run off or something makes this a false time period.

"All of you listen to me. David's being here has created a change in the overall time continuum and as a result this time he is in will cease to exist when he leaves. David is here only for a short time and then he will go back to his time and will continue his life. In thirty years, you will be here and have had a full and complete life with your mother and father. Do you understand?"

I was stunned, and as I looked around at the others, I could see they were as well. No one could say a thing; we sat there trying to grasp what he had said. If I understood him, I was still in my own time and I was here only for a short period of time and my being here thirty years in my future left my children without their father during that thirty years period.

"No, No, No, this is not right. Professor you're all screwed up in this thing. What you're saying is dad has made a time jump to this time period for some reason and he will, after a set time period, return to his time frame and we will become his future in thirty years?"

"That's right Lisa. Listen to me. Something serious happened in 2015 that is relevant and important to us here in 2045. What that is he knows, and we just have to get it out of him in the time we have left. Oh, by the way, don't take that watch off anymore. Every time it re-synchronizes it cuts our time down.

"I don't know how much time we have but we need to dedicate our time to this thing and do it now. Again David, what was going on in 2015 we cannot find in the records here in 2045 we need to know about now?"

"Professor, there is another problem and that is the voice I experienced last night. If what you are saying is true then that voice was real and it was trying to get me to remember what I knew or what I know."

I was starting to understand, the professor was right, there was a reason and it all had to do with me. Why this was happening this way I had no idea, but it was something tied the years 2015 and 2045 together and it was important.

Damn, I wanted to get up and run out the front door and not stop running until I dropped dead. He was asking me for something, and I had no idea what it was. But now I knew it was there and was driving me nuts.

Some event or happening that took place then is vital for me and my family now in 2045. "Damn Professor, I don't know. I can't think of anything that was of a major issue that day thirty years ago. I know it was just yesterday for me, but I'm at a loss as to what it is, you're looking for."

We were at a loss as to what to do next. There was something important going on in 2015 in or around Bradford, Pennsylvania that I needed to remember. In some way it was going to be important to the people living in Bradford in 2045.

Everything had changed. This was no longer just a Jacobs family issue; it was beyond that and would impact the whole of the community in the time period we were involved in right now. The problem was just what the hell was it?

Now it was no longer me wondering what had happened to me. No, it was me being here for a reason. It was something so important the fabric of time had been bent and violated in order for me to be here and identify it and or correct it, if it was possible.

Finally, the Professor pulled his computer out of its case and set it on the coffee table. Then he looked at me. "All right we're going back and take a look at that June day in 2015 and see if we can find anything that touches you or brings about a reaction."

I had no idea if he was on the right track but at least we were doing something positive. As I waited for him to bring the computer on line I started to think about yesterday and what it was that could have been so important it would cause this type of a process to try and overcome or counter it.

At the time I was an engineer for a developmental and planning group. Our main areas of expertise were in transportation technology. I was currently involved in the development of a new Super Train that was being designed. The hopes were this train would be the one selected to be used in the expanded railroad system that was being implemented across the country.

Needless to say, the project was secret and involved one hell of a lot of money. My particular part of the project was the main drive engine. At the speeds the train would be moving, the engine would have had to handle unbelievable amounts of force as it produced the power to drive the train. That in turn brought up the issue of the drive wheels and their ability to handle the force loads the engine would produce. Because of our preliminary studies we determined the wheels would not work on this train.

We then considered a magnadrive system. As we worked through the magnetic technology available at the time, we began to understand we would need something more advanced. Something that would result in significant power generation and be able to produce the needed power at the most cost-effective level possible.

We found it, but it was something dangerous and could impact the whole of the earth if we lost control of it. Actually, Albert discovered it. Albert is one of those guys you look at and think this character couldn't walk ten feet without tripping over his own feet. He had glasses so thick if he dropped them the impact would crack the floor.

He was the original meek and mild man, the original geek. He believed just about anything you told him and as a result he was the brunt of more jokes than you could imagine. He took it all in good humor, but at times I could see a glint of hurt there.

I liked Albert a lot and as a result we got along well. If no one else knew it I knew this man was just a fiber short of being a true genius. I would learn shortly he was in fact a genius and much more. I would learn he had in his mind the means of controlling the whole of the world and every living human being on it. A bold statement yeah, but it was a true statement as well.

"You know what it is, now work with it."

The thought shot through my brain like a bullet and I knew it was the voice from last night. I was there, but not quite sure just what it was I was zeroing in on. It had to be Albert and our project, but I still could not touch the one thing that would fire all my memories.

Suddenly I stopped my line of thought. I looked at the professor and started to shake my head. He knew instinctively something was going on. "David, what is it?"

It was hitting me I had not even considered what my life was thirty years ago, that is, until right this moment. "I don't understand. I haven't thought about what I was yesterday until right now and I was." I stopped and looked at everyone around the table. "No, that couldn't be, how could I not know what my profession was until just now?"

I stopped and sat there looking at the table when I felt Lisa take hold of my hand. "Dad, what is it?" she was leaning forward and looking up into my face. "Dad what just happened, what were you thinking?"

I was feeling sick and light headed as she sat there trying to get me to answer her. God, I was involved in something so bizarre I was having a hard time actually thinking it, let alone verbalizing it.

Just then the professor came over to me and grabbed me by the shoulder and shook me. "David, snap out of it. We don't have time for you to crap out on us right now."

I looked at him and then shook my head and stood up and pulled away from Lisa and the professor and walked across the room.

When I turned and looked at them, all I saw were four people trying to deal with the insanity of this moment and the freak they had among them.

The professor walked over to me. "David, I can see something serious has happened to you. Something you have remembered and that something must be verbalized to the rest of us, do you understand?"

He stood there waiting for me to answer him. "Yeah, I understand professor, but this is something so crazy, so monstrous I'm not sure I can communicate it to you accurately and intelligently.

"Professor, you're right when you say something in 2015 has happened that will impact you here in 2045. The problem sir is I'm that something and I'm here now and the impact has arrived."

He got this blank look on his face as he stood there looking at me. "David, are we too late?"

"I don't know professor, but I do know it's here and it's not going away. I don't know if I can change it or intercede in it, but if I don't my future and the future of my children will be killed right here in 2045. In our normal time frame we will move right into it and the end will be a simple flicking of a switch and all will cease to exist."

Now I was really sick because everything was coming back to me. It was all there, every second and every action that would bring all things to an end when the future reached this point. Shit, we had managed to kill the world and knew nothing about it.

No, wait, we did and it was Albert who had the key. Albert knew and they hauled him off to some place for safe keeping. Those dumb fools had taken the one being that had the answers and took him away to hide him. "No, they couldn't have done that. Damn it anyway, those fools have screwed this whole thing up."

By now the other three were moving toward me. "Dad, for the love of God what is going on?" Lisa was standing directly in front of me and holding my hands.

Finally, I pushed the professor back to the coffee table and directed the others to sit down. "All right, here it is. What I'm going to tell you now is the whole issue. I don't know what we can do from here, but at least you're going to know what is happening.

"What has keyed this whole mess was the professor wanting me to go back to my time and think of everything outside of what I was centering on, my life and you, my family. When I did, I effectively covered up my other life, the rest of my living activity at that time.

"You see I'm an engineer. I would have thought the three of you had known that, but apparently that has been blocked in you as well. That tells me this time frame I'm in is not fully the true time frame for 2045. It means to me 2045 is still in the making stages and it can be reworked and redesigned to meet the happening that came before it.

"Anyway, I'm an engineer and I have been working on a top-secret propulsion system for a new train my company is designing. If successful that train will be able to travel between Los Angeles and New York, about twenty-five hundred miles, in three hours.

"The design of the machine all depended on the power plant Albert and I were working on. Oh, Albert is my partner at the design institute. Albert is the genius who came up with the power plant design and once he was done the company decided he needed to be protected so they hauled him out of there and hid him someplace.

"When they did that, they took the primary brain we needed off the project and created the situation that would result in the issues here in 2045. You see the propulsion system Albert came up with was based on a combination of plasma and magnetism. Through the use of a configured magnetic vortex, we could shoot a plasma beam into the vortex and the amount of power that was generated was as near too astronomical as you could get. By that I mean it was infinite.

"The company felt it needed to protect its mind trust and they hauled Albert off to some unknown place and left the rest of the design process to myself and the rest of our team. The problem is, or was, we did not know all the nuances of his design. We had no idea as to just what was needed to control the new power generator. We could build it and add controls to it, but as it turned out we could not completely control it.

"That meant under the right circumstances the power plant could go into a head long power generation mode and continue to build and produce power at an exponential rate until it hit a point of instability at which time the vortex would start to grow. If we could not control the vortex it would continue to grow and, in the process, eat everything within its ever-increasing range. In effect it could eat the earth."

I sat there looking at them and shaking my head. The rest of them were almost lifeless the way they were watching me. "Kids, the system continued on a fast track to production and the building of the system from Los Angeles to New York with other destinations to come later. That system was designed to come right through Bradford, Pennsylvania.

"The significance of Bradford is, this is the place where the power plant will go out of control and produce the vortex. Bradford will be the first community to die under the effects of the vortex."

The professor was looking at me intently. "David, you're telling us your engineering team has designed and is building a machine with an advanced power generating system in it that, if not properly controlled, can produce this vortex that could destroy the world?"

"Yes Professor, that's exactly what I'm telling you. But the issue is even more difficult than that. The control of the vortex is in the mind of Albert and unless we can find him and get him back to the team this thing will happen."

"But David, haven't you told the company heads about this?"

"Professor, we have and they either don't believe us or don't care. The point is they have determined Albert is a valuable property and they are going to protect that property and glean anything and everything they can out of him no matter what it costs."

Finally, Patrick stood up. "Then what we need to know is where this Albert is, is that right?"

I sat there looking at him and then it hit me. Hell, yes that was the key and I was now in a place that was after-the-fact in Albert's disappearance. With a little work we should be able to locate where and when Albert came back into the public picture.

I looked at Pat. "You're right, we need Albert and this may be the time to go back and find him. All we need to be able to do is locate where they have him stashed. Once I have that we can then go back to 2015 and find him and get him back on the project.

"I'm not sure what it's going to take to locate him, but at least we'll know where he is. That should also give us the names of those people who have hid him away. Once we identify them, we can determine their overall motives."

Yeah, I had known what I was there for and now I wish I didn't. I knew exactly what was coming and when it was coming and it was just hours away. I didn't tell them because it would have put too much undue pressure on them at a time when I needed them the most.

With that we set to work. The Professor, Pat and I set to work on the computer and started to track anything and everything about Albert from 2015 till now here in 2045.

The girls went to work on Jane's computer looking for the development, construction and implementation of the new Super Train.

As I sat there, I started to think more on the nature of the project and its projections. I finally came up with what I wanted. I turned to the girls. "Listen, when we set up the developmental schedule for the train, we had determined the infrastructure of the system would take twenty-five years to complete. That means you should find something on the train five or six years ago. Understand?"

They both nodded and then settled into finding the information we would need. Meanwhile the Professor and Pat were working on Albert. They had gone back to 2015 and then started working toward now. It was in 2020 when they found the next reference to Albert. He appeared at an international conference in Zürich, Germany. At the time he was presenting a paper on the Vortex Plasma Generation System. It was clear at the time he was under close security coverage.

As I watched the news video of his presentation, I noted he was not the Albert I had known. No, this Albert was more polished and more of a showman.

I looked at Pat. "That's not Albert. That person is a look-a-like. His personality comes nowhere close to how Albert was. They have him stashed and working and then are having this guy act the part for the public.

"He has to be a scientist and have a background in plasma and electromagnetic concepts. Those aren't topics that just any old look-a-like could deal with, especially in a conference such as that one. That means this person is special as well and we should be able to track him without too much difficulty."

Pat turned back to the computer. "All right, we know this guy is an imposter and that gives us an opportunity to follow him and see where it takes us. Our problem is to try and determine who he actually is."

We then started to track Albert through his action over the next couple of years. They were showing this guy everywhere and anywhere. It became clear they were building an interest and a demand for the Super Train. But it still did not give us any indication as to where Albert was. I was starting to get a feeling we would not find him in time and if and when we did, it would be too late.

It was maybe twenty-five minutes later; the girls came up with the information we wanted. Lisa waved at me. "Dad, we have something here."

I went over to their computer and sure as hell there stood Albert by the developmental engine that was completed in 2020. This one was Albert, but he looked a little drawn and haggard. "Yeah, that's Albert alright. I can tell by the way he stands. His shoulders are hunched and he is leaning to his left. That's the way he has always been for as long as I've known him.

"All right, where was that photo taken? We need to know what the article is all about."

Jane started to read out loud. "The International Conglomerate is building the first cross-country Super Train has introduced the first prototype of the primary engine that will be the power for this new train.

"The lead designer of the train, Mr. Albert Aberdeen, is standing at the front of the train. He is pointing out the train will have no wheels and will in fact ride on a cushion of electromagnetic energy. When asked what the main power system was, he deferred that to the project coordinator.

"This project has a startup or initial testing schedule for service between Los Angeles and New York in 2045. The train will run in a tube or tunnel that will be maintained at a vacuum which will reduce or eliminate any air resistance while it is running.

The first run will be a break-in run and will not be at the speeds the train will ultimately be capable of. Mr. Aberdeen felt the initial run will take around ten to twelve hours and if it's successful then subsequent runs will increase in speed.

"Eventually they foresee speeds moving up into the area of five hundred miles per hour range which would make the run between the two cities around five hours. If it's successful then they would work on up to its ultimate and planned speed of eight hundred miles per hour.

"When asked if our current railroad system could handle those speeds Mr. Aberdeen advised a new system is in the making at this time. That new line will be dedicated to the Super Train. He advised the new line for the Super Train could not run-on normal rail tracks. The new system would be a tube that would run underground about a hundred to one hundred fifty feet.

"He also advised, as he had said before, the tube would maintain a vacuum thereby decreasing the level of resistance the train would have to overcome.

"When asked where the line was going in, he could not address the issue advising us he was responsible for the power plant and main engine and the actual rail line was being worked on by someone else. We would have to ask the project director for that information.

"One thing he was able to tell us was the new line would not run in the same corridor as current lines. Because of the speeds involved this new line would have to be dedicated and separated from all other rail traffic."

As she finished, I felt the sting of understanding setting in. "Did you get that?" I asked the professor. "Albert said the project would launch its first run in 2045, this year."

The professor came over to the table and looked at me. "All right David, where was the main system going to be assembled and then where was the first run going to start?"

I stopped and thought about the question. I had been oblivious as to what my past was until just a short time ago and now everything was starting to jell. I still had a maelstrom of questions inundating me and I had to work my way through all the thoughts that were charging through my mind.

Clearly, when I made the jump to this time, it had affected my memory and as each new fresh set of facts came up, they brought with them a massive number of additional questions. Right now, I needed to push my way through all the chaff and get to the basic facts of this situation.

I was involved in something that was earth changing and possible earth killing. For some reason I was set or dumped into the future as a means of addressing the potential disaster this new train could wreak on the world if we did not act and act fast.

On top of all that, how the hell were we going to make the move that could stop or at least slow down the first real test of the new train? So far everything has ended up in the form of a question, so let's take a look at the questions that are before us.

First of all, how did I get here in 2045?

Second what was the purpose of me coming to this time frame?

Third, what is my actual position in the development and planning of the new Super Train?

Fourth, where is Albert Aberdeen?

Fifth, what part is Albert playing in this thing anyway?

Sixth, how much time do we have before something disastrous happens in relationship to the Super Train?

Seventh, will I be able to return to my past and regain my life as I knew it then?

Eighth, can we actually stop the disaster from happening here in 2045 or do the actual actions needed to stop it have to take place in 2015?

There may be other issues but to me right now this was it. I now knew the professor was right and I was here for a specific time period and then I would return to my time. Not knowing what my time schedule was, we had to work fast and hard to get everything done before the return process took effect.

A feeling of hopelessness washed over me as I sat there looking at the others. I could see the realization of the magnitude of this issue setting in on everyone and it told me we needed to get to work and get to work now.

I looked at everyone. "All right we have come up with a number of questions concerning this situation and the first question is how I got here. As I think about it, I have a feeling my dream from last night is far more important than I thought it was.

"There is something that brought me here, some process or mechanical means that took me out of one time period and dropped me into another. We know two things, first of all I passed through some barrier that made the physical jump happen. Second, there appears to be someone or some other being involved in my time jump."

The professor was nodding his head. "Yes, I think you are right and I also think we need to know the connection between those two events and what is happening now.

"David, I believe you will need to make contact with that being in some way. You have to find out who or what it is and then determine if it can help us. It would also be nice if we could find out when the vortex is supposed to happen."

Yeah, I knew he was right and I also knew the time I came from had the keys for dealing with the problem we were facing in this time. Somehow, I needed to pull the two time periods together and then get oriented so that what had happened in 2015 could be related directly to what was happening in 2045. The key was 2015, everything was there.

CHAPTER SIX

Back to 2015

Right now, we needed information and the best source of that information was the year 2015. Somehow, I needed to get back to that time and then trace the Super Train process in detail. The only way I was going to be able to do that was through my memory and right now I didn't trust my memory at all.

I turned to the professor. "Paul, I need to find some way to open up my memory for the time around 2014 and 2015. I need to return to my job and remember in detail what was going on then and what I, in particular, was doing at the time. Right now, I'm finding it hard to remember even the simplest things. I need to be able to bring details back, details we desperately need."

Paul sat there a minute and then slapped both of his knees with both hands and stood up. "David, are you willing to let me do a drug induced memory search?"

A drug induced memory session? Now that was an idea, the problem was, could I handle it and especially here in 2045? "Paul, we need something to bring the information out. My only problem is whether it will work under these circumstances.

I'm actually here on a time jump basis and I'm worried when I made the jump my memory didn't jump in total with me. Can I actually carry out that process and still survive or remain here? Or even more important, can we trust what my memory recalls under a drugged condition?"

Paul listened to me intently and then shrugged his shoulders. "David, that I'm not sure about. Yes, you are in a time jump and we believe it was a forced jump. But even if it was, you are still physically here. That tells me you could go through with the drug induced process and it would work. However, I fear it may be more dangerous than if it was done to a resident of this time."

All right, there it was. I could try and the need was there and the results could tell us one hell of a lot about this whole mess. There was a risk, and the question was if I was willing to try it. The answer to that was actually rather simple. "Yeah Paul, I'll do it. We have to have the information and we need it now, so let's do it."

The professor had to leave for about an hour while he went to his office and picked up the drugs needed to carry out the process. While he was gone the rest of us sat down to talk over the coming event. "Now I want you three kids to know I really appreciate the fact this whole thing has been most difficult for you.

"What I wanted to say to you is when this process starts, I have no idea just what is going to take place. My hope is we can open up my mind and let my memory release and determine what I have been involved in back in 2015. Now when my memory comes back, you need to know things are going to change. Let me explain to you what I mean.

"When I came here to this time, your time was set and functioning. Do you agree?"

They all three nodded their heads and agreed.

"During my time here, my memory has been developing and we now know I am here by some means other than an accident. It means I still do not know who brought me here and how it was done. But I was placed here by some means and by someone.

"As my time here continues and my memory starts to come back, I think there are going to be some changes in the thirty-year time period that stands between my time in 2015 and your time here in 2045.

"Now listen to me, you are going to have to be aware of what is taking place. You are going to have to be prepared to take steps in dealing with any changes that may manifest themselves here in this room at this time as my memory brings out more and more of what the past has been. Those past memories could clearly change things here and now.

"I'm not sure if I have to speak those memories that manifest themselves here in me at this time, in your time frame. It may be as my mind opens up to any new memories that alone could bring about the changes. I will ask the professor to take it slow and easy. With each question we will need to include a time of waiting so we can discern any changes that may come before they are cataclysmic."

Lisa raised her hand. "Dad, are you saying your remembering could be harmful or dangerous for us?"

I sat there trying to think of the best way I could say this to her. "Lisa, what I am saying is we are delving into the unknown here and when we do there can be and probably will be reactions we did not anticipate. Now let me say this, it could be time is set and everything that has happened between 2015 and 2045 is going to be the same no matter what I do, whether I came here or not. I just do not know.

"That raises the question as to whether we can stop this thing, this Super Train. If time is set and cannot be changed then everything I have said, done and gone through will change nothing. If that is the case then I may never go home to my time in 2015. I may simply cease to exist and you will have lived the past thirty years wondering where your father went so long ago.

"I know this, I came here for a purpose, I'm in a Time Trap that will either kill me or I'll be successful and we will deal with the Super Train thing. I now know, I sense, if I'm successful I would return to my time frame and would live my life out and you kids would have a father during the time between 2015 and 2045. I also sense if things go bad, if I were to die here and now then what you have lived these past thirty years will not change.

"To me the decision was obvious. I came here because of you kids, your mom and the need to deal with the Super Train issue. However, this thing happened, whoever brought me here knew when I got here, I would be missing from 2015 on or until I returned to my time and my life continued on. I guess I've answered the question as to whether time is static or can change. Clearly it can change, clearly it is not static."

Everyone became quiet. We were looking at a situation no one had ever faced before. When I had been pulled from 2015, at that very moment everything for my children had changed. I jumped thirty years and during that thirty year jump they continued to live their lives after having their father disappear.

I landed here in 2045 and they had progressed day by day and hour by hour to this point. I made the jump in seconds and they lived the jump in years. When I walked through the door at the police department everything changed. It not only changed it turned into a nightmare.

Each had aged thirty years and I had aged only as long as it took me to make the jump, only seconds. In the process, I had shot across time having no experience of the time period and landed right there in front of them. I know I had a problem with that, but I couldn't even imagine what they felt and were going through.

That alone would be enough for any one rational human being to deal with, but now we're, I'm, asking them to go along with me in the quest for the truth, not knowing where this could lead.

Here I am from thirty years in the past messing around with their time frame or continuum and we expect no repercussions. Oh boy, there were going to be repercussions, there had to be. You can't mess around with time in this manner and not expect a reaction.

So far that reaction has been related to me and the impact of the jump on me and my mental welfare. But when I start to carry out activities within their time continuum then just about anything could and would probably happen.

Then it touched me, if I were successful in dealing with my reason for being here and then returned to my time continuum then this past thirty years of their lives would have never happened and they would be back in 2015 living their life with their father present. That had to be my goal.

Whatever I did here it had to be of such a level of success I could return to my time and erase all they have been living here in their time. God, what a hell of a mess this has turned out to be.

Just then the professor came through the door. As he set his case down, I related to him what I had just said to the kids and my memory had opened up some more. He was nodding his head. "Good, that means your memory is actually coming back and we don't have to force it. All we need to do is accelerate it a bit and hopefully it will come back in full force and give us what we need."

We were at a critical time and I knew I had to get my memory back in full. I did not understand why it was this way, but I knew if we could correct it, I had to give it a try. It then dawned on me. "Paul, what about the being I experienced in my sleep last night, how will that fit into this overall situation?"

He stopped emptying his case and stood up. "You're right, I had forgotten all about that. If there is another involved in this process then it must have used some method or methods to get you to this time. If it used drugs then the application of these drugs could be dangerous. It could generate an entirely different set of issues that could kill any attempt by us to deal with the Vortex issue."

He sat down and ran his right hand through his hair. "David, this is going to be your call. You're the one taking the risk."

Damn, I was looking at the professor not really knowing what I wanted to say or do when Lisa came over to me. "Dad, what if you tried to contact the being who put you here? What if Paul gave you something to put you to sleep, would it be possible you would then meet up with this other being again?"

I had forgotten about the fact I made contact when I was asleep. I knew she was right. I didn't like it, but it was the way to go. I turned to Paul. "She's right Paul. I need to sleep and then I need to find that other being and get this thing worked out. I don't want to, but I know I have to and I also know I'm ready."

111

Paul was busy writing a number of things down and then he stood up. "I agree, we will give you a simple sleeping solution and let you go to sleep. The question is, do we have to do it at Lisa's or can you sleep anywhere?"

I walked over to the couch and sat down looking at Paul. "Paul, it makes no difference where I'm at. When I go to sleep the connection will be made. Don't ask me how I know, I can only tell you I know. So, give me the solution."

It took him five minutes to put it all together and then he brought it to me. I drank it down and settled back against the back of the couch and waited. Lisa sat down beside me and Pat and Jane sat down across the coffee table from me. The professor stood by my side and kept a check on my vitals as I started to nod off.

This was impossible. I was going to try and go to sleep and then make contact with this other being. The problem was if I'm asleep that means my mental process has shut down and I have no conscious capabilities. I was beginning to feel this would not, nor could it ever produce the end results we were looking for. Well, it was too late anyway. I had taken the drug and sleep was coming.

I felt the darkness wash over me as I slipped in to a sleep state. There was nothing there. I noted my mind was active and attentive so I waited. That in itself was odd. I was physically asleep and yet my mental capabilities were on line and functioning. I have no idea how long it was before I felt the presence. "Are you there?"

Whatever the hell it was doing, I knew it was doing it. I realized it was clearly in control and aware of my presence and what I was dealing with. Physically my body had gone to sleep, but mentally I was still active and in control. Clearly this was all part of the Time Trap or time continuum situation I was in. It had to be.

It was quiet and I was getting ready to ask again when it came. "Yes, I'm here."

"You know what is happening here don't you?"

"Yes, David I do. That's why I brought you here."

"Who are you?"

"David, you know who I am. Just think about it for a few seconds, it'll come to you."

I was supposed to know who this was, and if I thought about it, it would come to me. Why didn't it just tell me? Why all the guessing games? I was getting frustrated, I needed the information and I needed it now and this thing, whatever it was, wanted to play games.

"Look you, whatever you are or whoever you are, I don't need these games. I need information and I need it now."

"David, your mind is not at full operational levels yet for me to give you what you want or need. David, you have to function. You have to get that mind of yours to start to think and analyze what is happening, I can't do it for you. Let loose David, you know who I am and why you're here."

All right, I needed to apply myself. First of all, I needed to relax and let my mind open up. It's just like when we were dealing with problems with the project when Albert would tell everyone to relax and open up our minds and think.

I stopped mid thought. "Albert, is that you?"

"Good for you David. I knew you would figure it out. Now we can get things moving and deal with this mess we've made."

"What the hell do you mean by 'Mess we've made.' anyway?"

"David, we, everyone on the team and in management has made this thing that is coming at this world. In the push to make this project work, we set issues aside, always keeping our eyes on the big picture and never looking at the small bothersome issues that came along.

"As we progressed, the management became more and more paranoid toward outside involvement in our project and the possibility of industrial espionage. As a result, they took me and slipped me out of the project and into a place of protection. In effect they have kidnapped me.

"David, there has been so much money dumped into this project they will not listen to me when I tell them this Super Train is doomed and the resulting effects from the failure of the train will destroy the world.

"David, they are no longer listening to reason. Everything is the bottom line; the money being spent and the potential income that may result. David, we have to stop this project and it needs to be done today, 2045."

What the hell was going on anyway? I just discovered Albert was the being responsible for bringing me here to the year 2045. But how the hell did he do it? There was something really wrong and I was no closer to finding out just what the hell it was than I was yesterday.

"Albert, what's going on here anyway? There is more to this than just the Super Train and I think you know?"

There was a silence as I waited there in the darkness for an answer. He was there with me; I could feel him. I then felt a touch in my mind and he spoke. "David, you are the closest person I had back there in 2015. When everyone else was treating me like some oddity you treated me like an equal. I brought you here because I felt I needed your help in cleaning up this Super Train danger.

"David, I am going to destroy the train but I haven't decided just how I am going to do it. If I let the vortex develop it will kill the world. I have been mulling that idea over and find it to be favorable. I hate the world and everything it stands for. This world let the likes of these business giants come into existence and then subjugate the rest of mankind by their monetary domination.

"I hate what they did to me, and I find all I want is revenge. All I want is to see every one of them die and realize their greed was the responsible act that brought about this disaster.

"David, over the past thirty years they have held me in isolation, not letting me out to be as others, but trying to retain and control my mind. Well, just the reverse has happened. My mind has expanded and grown and now I can control time and I can control the present. I can make the Super Train go into a vortex or I can just destroy the train and bring all those behind this monster to total monetary bankruptcy."

Man was I in the wrong place and the wrong time. It was Albert alright, but he was crazy as hell. If what he was telling me was true, he had changed while they held him in isolation and that change was a mutation of his mind. If he was telling me the truth, he could control time and space and everything that functioned within it. I realized I was in a trap; a Time Trap and it was controlled by Albert.

117

"Albert, I don't know what to say. I knew they had taken you off the project. When I tried to check on you and where you were, they threatened me. The fact is they sat me down in an office and told me flat out I either forgot about you or I would pay and so would my family."

"David, I know they did that. I found out about fifteen years ago what they had done to you. At first, I had thought you had been in on their actions in kidnapping me, but by chance I was able to glean the knowledge you were treated almost as badly as I was. David, I hold nothing against you. In fact, the one thing that is keeping me from creating the vortex is you and your family."

I must have been moving around or something because I felt someone shaking me. I reached out to Albert and he came back to me. "Go David, they need to talk to you. I'll be waiting here for you when you come back."

I woke up with the four of them leaning over me. Lisa was saying. "Dad, wake up. Come on Dad we need you to come back. Wake up."

I let go of Albert and slowly opened by eyes. Once they saw my eyes open, they all moved back and Paul stepped in front of me. "David, are you, all right?"

I sat up and looked at the four of them. "What's going on?"

"David, you were going into seizures. We were afraid you would have a heart attack and so we decided to wake you. David, what was going on?"

I sat there a minute and then asked everyone to sit down. "All right, I have some answers but you're not going to like them."

Paul was the first to respond. "What's going on David?"

I was sitting there thinking over what I had just experienced. It was Albert, he was the reason for my being there and it was him who was controlling the disaster we were looking at. How was I going to tell these people everything would depend on me and them as to whether Albert actually initiates the vortex or simply destroys the Super Train?

I slowly repositioned myself and looked at each of them, I had something to say. "You need to know I have found out what is going on, and I can tell you it's not good.

"I did make contact with the being that brought me here and this being is none other than Albert Aberdeen."

You could see the reactions setting in. Shock! Yeah, I would say so, but what was even more evident was the anger washing over the kids. Jane was the first to react. "How the hell could that be?"

I was shaking my head and continued. "Albert has gone through a mutation, his word not mine. In addition, I have to say I'm sure he is here right now with us and knows what we are saying and feeling. I caution you not to be too critical or damning of him. Please let me finish before you pass any judgments.

"Albert was my partner in the preliminary design of the Super Train. I have to say I was more his helper because of the fact Albert is without a doubt a genius. I knew at the time and I know now he was much more than that. He was a brain trust that was worth more than all the gold in Fort Knox.

"It was his mind that designed and built the Super Train and I can tell you he was my best friend and still is. They took him away from the project and when I tried to find out what they did with him they threatened me and the welfare of my family. I was forced to abandon any attempts at finding Albert because of those threats against you and Helen.

"Albert knows that and his hate for the powers to be is beyond description. He is the one planning or thinking of creating the vortex and bringing about the disaster that would result. His one and only problem is me and you, and that is keeping him from making that terrible move.

"What I am telling you is we, you and I, hold the key to stopping this from happening. Paul, Albert is mad. I mean he is angry and ready to take payback against those who have held him captive all these thirty years.

"The power of that man is beyond anything you or I can comprehend. He was able to reach back thirty years and pull me out of my time period and bring me here to this one. A mind that can do that can create the vortex and can destroy this world.

"Paul, I need to go back to sleep so I can continue to talk to Albert and make a determination as to just what it is, he wants to do. Paul, you have to keep me in that state and not jump the gun if my body starts to act up. Albert needs me and he needs me now without any interruptions. If this kills me and it helps him keep from creating the vortex then my family will live and that's all I want."

Everyone sat there looking at me. I could see disbelief and fear running through them at that moment. They were part of something they had not known nor understood. I needed to give them a chance to ask the many questions were running through their minds. "All right what do you think?"

Pat stood up and started pacing. "Dad, I'm sorry, but to me it sounds like this Albert is crazy, crazy as hell. How do you know you can trust him?"

Pat was right. "Pat, I have no choice but to trust Albert. First of all, he has never ever let me down in the past. I know that man and when he says he is going to do something he means it and he will honor everything he says.

"Second, Albert and I have walked through a lot of fires over the years before 2015. He has always covered my back and I the same for him. Albert is not a superman. He is a small unassuming man with a mind that far out strips any other mind around or near him. Pat, I would and will trust my life to him."

"That's well and good dad, but we're not just talking about your life here, we're talking about everyone else's lives, us and the people of this world."

"Yes, I agree with you, but don't you see the key here. It's Albert's feelings toward me that will make the difference for you and everyone else.

"I think we are going to have to team up with Albert to make his desires at revenge come true. I think we're going to have to assist him in gaining his freedom from those who are holding him. Kids, Albert needs to be free and we're the ones who will have to see to that."

Just what the hell we were getting into remained to be seen, first of all my relationship with Albert was a mental one and only when I was asleep. We still had no idea where he was at and what he was actually doing. We would need to determine his location and just how we were to go about gaining his release.

In addition, I was sure this thing was real, but what if it wasn't. What if I was having a nightmare and all this was not real, was not happening. After all, if Albert could be the one making me jump time periods then

123

I could just as well be dreaming this whole nightmare.

There was only one problem and it was a big one. I was physically here. No, it's not a dream but I'm physically here in 2045. There is no way I could imagine all I have seen and witnessed so far. In no way could I anticipate and create the appearance and age of my children, the actions and facility of the police, the shopping and the stores we went to.

No, we were dealing with a man who has, in some way, manifested into something beyond human. Though I did not see him, I could feel him and it was something I fear seeing if and when we are able to free him.

What I knew right now was I needed to go back to sleep and continue my contact with Albert. I turned back to Paul. "All right Paul, I need to return to Albert and continue our exchange. As far as my physical wellbeing goes, I think you're going to have to let me be and try and counter anything physical you're sure is a danger to me."

Lisa had started to stand and shake her head. "No, we're not going to do this." She was walking toward me and pointing her finger at Paul. "You are not going to throw your life away for this thing, do you understand me."

I reached out and took hold of her shoulders and started to shake her. "Lisa, listen to me. Paul is doing nothing to me. This is my decision and it's one that must be done. We have to know what Albert is up to and if we can stop the disaster that is coming down on this community. If we don't then you, your brother and sister and everyone else you know will die and I will not sit by and let that happen. Do you understand?"

She was starting to cry as I talked to her and then I pulled her close to me and held her. "Dad, we just found you and now this. I don't know if I can take this again, having you lost to us again."

I held her back from me and looked her in the eyes. "Lisa, don't you understand if we can help Albert and stop this disaster from happening, I will go back to my time and you will have never lost me. This time right now is not what it actually could be, it's what it became when he brought me here and when I go back it will go away and you will live a life that never lost me."

This was nuts, even as I explained it to her it sounded nuts, but I knew it was true. I was in a Time Trap and if I wanted my life back the way it was, I had to work with Albert and help him deal with the Super Train issue. There was no other way.

My most serious unknown was what Albert had mutated into. He had said he had mutated and he was not as he was. Did he mean that his brain had changed or his physical form had changed?

I had to condition myself to deal with whatever was coming. Something was telling me I did not want to see or meet Albert at this time.

I turned back to Paul. "All right Paul, I need to go back to sleep now and make sure it is more me sleeping and not the drug making me sleep, know what I mean?"

He was smiling. "Yes, I know what you mean. I will keep the dosage down so it just pushes you into sleep. Are you planning on trying to communicate with us while you're asleep?"

"Yeah, I would hope to be able to do that and I figure the lighter the dosage the more likely I will be able to communicate with you. Does that sound reasonable?"

"David, I think that under this circumstance it's more than reasonable. Are you ready to go?"

This was it. I felt I would be asleep for however long it was going to take me to find a solution. If Albert cooperates and helps me determine the best way to deal with the industrial powers, he is so angry with, then maybe I can stop this event from happening. "OK Paul, let's do this."

I had no sooner fallen asleep than I felt Albert's presence. "Albert, are you there?"

"Yes David, I'm here. Are you ready to assist me in dealing with those who have harmed me?"

He sounded like he was mad as hell. There was something there that told me Albert was not the Albert I knew. He was much angrier, almost to the point of illness. It was then I realized Albert was probably insane. I began to question my ability to deal with this, to deal with Albert in his sick state. "Albert is this process going to remain on a mind-to-mind basis?"

"David, I would prefer it that way. You may not want to see me after what they have done to me. Really, you don't want to see me."

127

My mind was seeing all kinds of odd and freaky visions of what Albert might now look like. No, I needed to meet with him person to person. I needed to see what I was fighting for and what they had done to him. "Albert, I don't like that idea at all. I would prefer to meet with you and talk to you person to person, one on one. Is that possible?"

There was silence, yet I could feel him considering my request. What the hell did they do to that man that would make him not want me to see him? I had a foreboding feeling surge through my body as I realized what they may have done was so damned far out there it would drive a good man insane.

He finally came back to me. "All right David, I will meet with you but it will not be a physical meeting. I will bring your mental being here to me and you will be able to see me and understand what is going on. David, listen to me, I'm going to trust you in this situation. I need you to stay with me and not let my appearance drive you from me. David, if that happens, I will surely destroy the world regardless of who it hurts."

Now things were starting to fall into place. Something has happened to this man that is so devilish, so mean he has gone insane and his whole existence is for one thing and that is revenge.

It was time to communicate with the others. "Paul, touch me if I am coming through." I felt a hand touch the back of my right hand one time. "Good I felt that one touch. I will be going with Albert to his physical location. I will remain physically here but he will be taking my mind to his location. As I go, I will keep communicating and you keep tapping my hand. Is that all right?"

There was another tap on my right hand.

I turned back to Albert. "All right Albert, I'm ready. What do you want me to do?"

"Nothing David, you will find yourself here in my chamber in just a few seconds. Please understand the lights are low and I will keep them at that level for several minutes until I'm ready for you to see me. Here we go."

I felt nothing at first other than it became quiet again. Then I started to feel a movement, well not actually a movement. It was more like a repositioning, like I was coming at something from a different

129

perspective. What I did know was this man somehow had mutated to the point he was capable of unbelievable mental actions and he was demonstrating that right now.

In just seconds I knew I was in a room, a chamber as he called it. It felt cool and yes it was dark. For the first time I felt like I was floating. Before I had felt like I was sitting on something or standing, but this feeling was that of floating.

I started to concentrate on my mental sight and trying to see what was around me. Even in the darkness, and it was not completely black, there was a light, a wisp of light around me.

The stark realization as to where you're at when it finally hits you is terrifying. It came to me almost like being punched in the gut. I was in water, well some liquid anyway. I immediately started to fear the thought of drowning and then realized I was here mentally and not physically, that was why he refused to let me come to meet him in the physical form.

I had been there waiting for I don't know how long. "David, how do you feel?"

"Albert, I'm doing fine. I did have a little start when I realized I was in water or some other liquid, is that right?"

"Yeah, David you have it right. This is the chamber they keep me in. It's my home, my permanent home."

Now things were starting to come together. There was no way he could live in this environment in the human body. No, No, that can't be. Damn them anyway. He has no body; they took him out of it and placed him here so they could control him. No wonder he's insane.

It was then the realization as to where I was washed over me. "Yes, David that is how they control me. They took my body and placed me in this tank. I had no means of leaving this place that is until my mind started to expand. David, it has reached a point where I can go anywhere, I want, either in this time frame or any other time frame. It is by this means I will take my revenge."

I knew I was in suspension there in that tank or whatever the hell it was, but I still could not see Albert or what Albert actually was at this time. It was then I noted movement ahead of me. What I was to see would scare the life out of me, something so terrible that it numbs the mind.

Whatever it was it was moving toward me. I knew this was all mental and I was not physically there, but still the sense that something beyond my understanding was there, coming right at me. I could feel the cold sweat pouring off of me.

I can't imagine what my body was doing because my mind was trying to run, trying to get away from this abomination that was coming toward me. "David, please you must control yourself and understand I can't do anything about this situation. They have stolen my body and have left just my brain and spinal cord. That is all that is left of me. This is what those animals did to me."

It took everything I had to control myself and calm myself. I thought I could feel someone placing cold compresses on my forehead, whether they were or not, it felt good. I watched this thing as it floated around me and then moved back to my forefront and stopped there. "Albert, what do you see when you position yourself here in front of me." I asked.

"David, I can see you as you are now. I also know your body is there on that couch in your daughter's living room.

"David, I see a power source, a glow that is about sixteen inches across. There is no representation of a physical nature, just your mental presence." He started to move around me again.

I stayed motionless and let him do all the moving around. "Albert, are you controlling my being here or am I in control. I feel I can move and come and go as I please, but still, I don't understand how I'm doing this."

He moved back in front me. "David, I am in control, but I have given you free movement because you're my friend and I know what it feels like to be controlled. It is my hope you can help me deal with these monsters who have done this to me."

"Albert, that's why I'm here, but I must tell you if you are still planning on creating this vortex with the intent of destroying the world, I cannot help you."

I didn't know if my declaration would cause any unforeseen reactions from him, but I had to be truthful with him.

He swung around and moved away from me maybe four feet and then turned back toward me. "David, I understand and I need to warn you I am in control here, not you. Everything I have had and dreamed of has been destroyed by those people and my hate is so deep I can only satisfy it by taking my revenge, total revenge."

We were at a critical point and I needed to press the issue but I also needed to restrain myself. The last thing I wanted was to set him off. His hate and anger were understandable, but his target was disproportionate. "Albert, I understand what you're saying and the fact is I agree with you.

However, I also disagree with you in that you plan on making every other man, woman, and child pay for something a few greedy people have done. Albert, this does not seem to be a justified action from my view of things.

"Listen to me. Those people who have done this to you deserve whatever you're planning for them, but the rest of the world's population has no idea as to what has happened to you or why it has happened. Do you see that?

134

"When you brought me here through your Time Trap that changed the future for my children, and when I got here, I was the long-ago lost father who had disappeared those thirty years ago and now I showed back up.

"Albert, my family went through thirty years of their lives never knowing where their father and husband had gone. Then I show up one day like nothing had happened. What the hell do you think that has done to them?"

He moved back toward me and stopped just inches away. "I never intended for that to happen. It was unexpected and hurtful and I know that. You have been my best friend, my brother, and I turned to you for help and in doing that I have hurt you and your family.

"But when I send you back everything will be reversed and will be back to normal for the next thirty years. Your family will know nothing of it."

"Albert, I will. You will send me back and I will live the next thirty years knowing this will happen and that is just not fair, not fair at all."

I could feel his remorse and anger at the same time. He was or appeared to change color right there in front of me. He had gone from a pink to a soft blue. "David, I don't know what to say. I had no idea what I did would work out this way. Believe me, I did not intend for it to go this way."

I felt myself reach out to him and touch his mind. "Albert, I know that. I can see the terrible thing that has been done to you, but only a few created this situation and only that few should have to pay.

"If you're after retribution, then it should be directed at those individuals and not the City of Bradford, this nation, or the world in general."

He said nothing and sat suspended there facing me. I wasn't sure whether I had taken the wrong step or he was just thinking over what I had said. It was clear to me this man had been severely treated over the past thirty years.

No wonder he was crazy, no wonder he was seeking revenge. He had finally, in all that time and isolation, developed the ability to exact his revenge through his mental capacity. That more than scared me, it was terrifying.

As time passed, I became more and more uncomfortable. It was obvious he was not going to respond to me now. "Albert, I need to go back to my kids and discuss what we have talked about here. Would that be all right with you?"

He didn't react. His color had gone to a redder red from the pink and I had a strong feeling he was angry and any attempt on my part to leave or pull back would not be permitted. I again asked for permission to return to the kids and finally he responded. I can only describe it in the form of sound. It was like his voice had mellowed and became softer.

The red changed back to pinker as he responded. "David, I need you here to assist me in the actions I must take. If you promise to return, I will permit it. However, if you lie to me and fail to return then our relationship is over and I will destroy that train and create the vortex effect. Do you understand?"

That was clear to me and I agreed, after all what was I to do? As long as I could keep him in a dialog, he was not doing anything harmful. I didn't know how long that would last, but I knew I had to keep trying. "I agree Albert, I would be a complete fool to fail to come to you and help you. Besides, you're my friend and that means everything to me."

"Thank you, David. You can go, but I will need you back here at the end of twenty-four hours. Agreed?"

I agreed and I felt him release me. I then gave the signal to Paul to pull me out of my sleep and I withdrew from Albert and his chamber.

CHAPTER SEVEN

The Challenge

As my head cleared, the four of them were standing over me each ready to pounce on me with all their questions all at once. Once I got everything into focus, I had to sit there and let the past event sink in and give myself time to make some sense out of what I saw and what Albert had said.

Finally, I looked at Paul. "Paul, he's crazy. What those people have done to him has driven him into insanity. I don't blame him but I know we are going to have to deal with him in some manner.

"You won't believe what I'm about to tell you, but I think the four of you need to know what I saw and what transpired between the two of us. This whole mess has taken

139

years to manifest itself and it's now at the breaking point.

"Albert wants retribution and he wants it in a big way. He wants total destruction of the world and all who live in it. I have managed to get him to think about all the innocent people who have no idea as to what has happened to him.

"It was those people; the heads of the company, who took that man, kidnapped him, in 2014 and put him away in a place where no one could find him. As they held him over the years, they were able to develop a system that would ensure he could never escape. They destroyed his body and all that remains is his brain and spinal column.

"He is in a tank of liquid where he has free movement around the tank but no way of getting out. If he did, he would never survive because the tank carries all the nutrients he needs to survive. Anyplace else would kill him.

"When they did that to him, he started to develop his mental capacity. As a result, he was able to move in time and find me and bring me here through his Time Trap. He wanted me solely because we were such close friends back then and we still are. He trusts me and needs me. I have agreed to help him. Just what I can do to help I don't know, but I did tell him the vortex was the wrong way to go. He didn't like that but is considering my argument against it."

The four of them had sat down by now and were unable to say anything or ask any questions. We sat there for several minutes when Paul asked. "Well, what are you doing back here? Clearly there must have been some agreement for him to let you come back?"

"Paul, there was. I promised to return in twenty-four hours if he let me come back. I told him I needed to see my kids and talk to them. That seemed to impress him and he agreed to my coming back.

"Now in twenty-four hours I will go back and by then we need to have some plan or process going that will help in stopping his making the vortex happen. Understand this; I don't think I can kill him. He is too powerful and would know my plan before I could make a move. Beside I don't want to kill him.

"So that leave us with one alternative to work toward and that is to assist him in his vendetta against those who did this thing to him. Now if that is what we are going to do, then we need to put this plan together so the four of you are not implicated. That means I need your input and with that we can formulate and then carry out whatever plan we develop.

"My point is I am not here. When this thing ends, I will be gone from this time frame and all they, the authorities in this time frame will find is a man that is in his mid-eighties and incapable of carrying out any action such as what needs to be done."

The magnitude of the issue was just starting to set in with the others when Lisa asked. "What will happen to Albert if and when this thing is carried out?"

"I don't know. He has not given me any indication as to what he plans for himself. I know that he does not want to stay in the tank for however long he will live, so I'm relatively sure he has a death wish. If he doesn't have a death wish then he has something else planned."

The professor was sitting there drumming his knees with his hand when he stood up. "Oh my God, he's planning on going back to 2015 with you. How, I don't know, but he is and if he does, he can change the entirety of the universe by his manipulation of time and space. Listen,

David, all of you, when David came here, he disappeared as he was in 2015 and showed up here. That changed the time continuum and with that he was a father who had just disappeared one day way back when and now suddenly reappeared.

"Now, when he goes back all that history, your history and not his, will change back, and David will be home with your mother and you kids. The next thirty years will never happen. A new and different thirty years will slide into place, that being your father being there with you. Are you getting what I mean?"

We were all nodding our heads.

"All right, now when your dad goes back what will change for Albert. Back in 2015 Albert had been taken or kidnapped, but his brain and spinal column were still in his body. That means everything that has happened in the past thirty years will no longer exist and Albert will then be able to reformate the year 2045 and all those years between.

"Albert wants to go back as he is now. He wants to move his mental capacity into 2015 and it will be then when he will take his retribution on those who have done this to him, before they can do it to him.

"When he returns to 2015 his body will be intact and his mental existence will infuse into his body in 2015. He has figured that out, and once he achieves that he will be mobile and capable of just about anything. Yes, he will still be insane."

Paul was right, and now this whole mess had just taken on an impossible air about it. Albert was not going to cause the vortex to happen at this time, he was going to go back to the beginning and build it into the system at that time. He was going to set this thing up so he had thirty years to manipulate and build his power base and then take over the entire system. What he planned after that I don't know, but I was sure I didn't want to know.

That explained my being here. He was going to use me as his mode of transportation back to 2015. Just how this was going to work I didn't know. All I knew now was he needed to get to 2015 and I was going to be his way there.

Things couldn't be anymore screwed up than they already were. We had twenty-four hours before I had to return to the tank and make some kind of a commitment to him.

I was sitting there thinking this mess over when it came over me. I suddenly realized there was much more to this than I had seen. I turned to Paul. "Paul, what if the whole specter of Albert was not true? I mean is it possible what I witnessed was actually a vision put in my mind by Albert and nothing close to what he actually is or looks like?"

I asked the question of Paul but everyone responded. The kids stood up and looked at Paul and then me. Paul was sitting there looking at the table top and thinking. He had a fearful look in his face. I had hit on something that was making an impact on the others, why I had no idea.

Paul raised his right hand and everyone settled back. "David, what they are reacting to is while you were asleep you made several comments. They were disjointed and made no sense at the time. What you just said made all that come together and it now makes sense.

"David, as you were dealing with Albert, we could hear you thinking out loud. By that I mean you were talking as if you were talking to yourself in your mind. One time you said. "He can't be serious." Next you said. "This is impossible, only a sick mind could think this up." Another time you

145

said. "He is truly insane and I can't trust anything he is saying.

"David, there are other comments that I wrote down, but the basics of everything you said was you could not believe what he said had happened to him actually did. Now you ask if the tank and the condition he was in could have been a vision he had placed in your mind and what you were seeing was a false vision.

"David, Albert is not being truthful with you. I think you're right when you say you think he is insane. I would venture to say he is not just insane but his insanity is dangerous. I think he's a paranoid schizophrenic and that is about as dangerous as you can get.

"David, I don't think you can go back to that meeting in twenty-four hours. There is something extremely dangerous going on here and I'm afraid Albert is right in the middle of it. Bottom line, I don't think Albert's appearance was any different than anyone else. What you saw was a projection or a vision and not the actual Albert. Why he did that I don't know, unless it was meant to show you the level of power he had reached."

"Paul, I can't avoid going back. The fact is he will be there no matter when I go to sleep. No, I have no choice in this matter. I must go back and I must do it within the twenty-four-hour period. I think it's important and we must stay with that schedule.

"Paul, the reason I'm here is that Albert brought me here and if he can do that then he can do just about anything. Now the question is, did he do it with his mind or was it by some mechanical or electronic process or system.

"Remember, Albert is a genius and he is capable of just about anything, but I feel what I saw was more a fantasy than a factual action. The important thing is we have made contact and we need to pursue it."

I was sure I had it pegged right, but we still needed to prepare for my return in twenty-four hours. If Albert can communicate with me in the manner, he did this time, then his mental capacity is off the charts. I had to keep in mind if his current condition was not true, but was a projection of what he thought, then I had to accept the fact that what I was seeing could just as well be the real thing.

It made little difference as to what was real or unreal. I needed to prepare and anticipate what was coming at our next meeting. The first thing we needed to address was my mental attitude. That, I felt and so did Paul, was critical for this next meeting. The issue was whether I was going to accept the brain and spinal cord thing or deny it. "Paul, what do you think about this tank and brain-spinal cord thing?"

"What do I think?" He was setting his note pad down and standing up. "David, I think it's phony as hell. From a scientific perspective I don't see how a person's brain and spinal column can be removed from the body and still survive.

"As far as I know there is no method or process which exists that will permit this type of action. The connection between the brain, spinal column and the rest of the body is so complex to try and separate any one part from the rest would kill everything. No, it is not a true picture of what is going on with him and I think you need to approach him in that way.

"Albert is clearly mentally damaged and he could well be a paranoid schizophrenic. But that condition will not give him the ability to carry out that kind of an act. His mind is fully developed and could do that whether mentally ill or not. I think what you witnessed was there for the shock value and nothing more.

"It was meant to do one of two things or both. It was to draw on your sympathy and it was to bring your anger out. If he can control those two reactions then he will have you on his side.

"How dare anyone do something like that to another human being? That would be the response he wants. Coupled with your anger, he would have a willing partner in whatever the hell it is he is planning."

That made sense, all the sense in the world and I was even more convinced what I had witnessed was in fact not true but a vision he imposed on my mind. Even at that it was one hell of a demonstration of his mental capabilities. That told me I still needed to be careful and aware as to what was going on and how his mental demeanor was holding up.

Meanwhile the kids had continued on their research into what could have happened to Albert. They had concentrated on the past sighting of Albert and the frequency of those sightings from the day he disappeared to the present. They were tracking thirty years of Albert and what they found was impressive.

My recall of when Albert disappeared determined he first came up missing in June of 2014. It was at the height of our developmental stage for the new Super Train. As I said before, Albert and I were working on the power plant for the train. It was during this process I became fully aware of Albert's mental capacity. In a word it was off-the-chart.

All the computations and preliminary engineering drawings had been completed. If what we had put down on paper actually worked it would change the history of mankind. Though it was being designed for the Train, its use could be applied in any situation where power was need to run something.

As we approached the time of his disappearance, I noted he was becoming more and more agitated. He started to snap at people and lose patience if anyone did not see things as he saw them. I had talked to him several times about it and he usually reacted by saying he knew that but he was just nervous and tired. It hadn't dawned on me there was something else behind his behavior.

When he came up missing and no one had any rational answer as to what was going on or where he was, I never thought about how he had been acting. I didn't tie the two things together.

In August of 2014 I had been to three meetings with the people in charge of the Super Train project and when the subject of Albert came up, they got rather defensive and tried to avoid the issue. I guess I was getting a little angry and started to press the issue when one day the director of the project called me into his office.

He was nervous as hell and couldn't sit still. I could tell this was not going to be a good meeting. He finally settled down and looked right at me. "David, since the day Albert came up missing you have been building a head of steam in trying to find out what happened to him. As a result, you are beginning to be one hell of a pain in the ass. Understand me?

"There isn't a meeting or discussion that takes place without you bringing up Albert's absence. That in turn keeps everyone else on edge and does not make things any better. The reason for you being here in this office is I must tell you to stop it. Stop this never-ending pursuit of Albert.

"No one here knows what has happened to him or why this has happened. David, you're talking to a bunch of people who have the same feeling and every time you bring that up its gut wrenching for them.

"David, you have to stop or I'll be forced to take steps I would hate to take. You just have to stop it. What you're doing is serving no purpose here and creating a lot of hard feelings and emotions. We don't need that.

"Now I'm going to leave this thing up to you. If you feel you cannot stop this never-ending questioning of everyone over Albert's disappearance then you will need to go. It's your decision and I want it right now. Not tomorrow, or a week, or a month. I want your answer right now. What's it going to be?"

Gees, the boss had never talked to me that way before nor had he ever laid anything on the line in that way. I felt my face flush and my temper jump. Hell, if he wanted to get rid of me, he should just fire me and get it over with. I felt like telling him that and then realized he was right. I was pushing the line and making a pest of myself. I had not realized how it was hitting everyone else.

Finally, I nodded my head. "You're right and I realize that now. It's the way Albert disappeared, he was such a close friend and I miss him so badly. No, I don't want to leave and I'll try to control myself in the future. I'm sorry if I hurt anyone's feelings. I just wanted an answer I could live with."

He was nodding his head back at me and then leaned across the desk toward me. "David, we all miss that little nut. There is not one of us who do not want to know what happened to him. It's just that we have a job here and we must continue. Listen, I don't want to sound to business like, but we do have a deadline to meet and this kind of activity that you've been displaying is not helping.

"Now, if it's all right I am going to believe you want to stay with us and the matter is closed. One thing I will give you and that is if there is any time you feel you need to talk about Albert then I will make myself available for you to ask questions or discuss ideas about why he is missing. Will that help?"

I was nodding my head and started to stand. I stopped half way up and looked at him and felt I needed to say something. I'm not sure what it was, but something told me to shut up, lay it down, and I stood up the rest of the way and walked away.

It was then I noticed his eyes and they were pleading for me to go, get the hell out of there and stay out. There was no doubt there was something going on and just then it stirred my mind and I knew there was not going to be an end to it. I would just have to stay low key.

That night after I had gotten home and Helen, the kids and I had eaten dinner the phone rang. I answered and a man on the other end asked. "Is this David Jacobs?"

"Yes, it is. Who is this?"

"David, you don't need to know my name. All you need to know is we know your supervisor talked to you today about dropping your inquiries about Albert Aberdeen. My purpose in calling you is to reinforce your understanding of what is at stake here. Mr. Jacobs, you need to know any further inquiries by you on the location or situation concerning Mr. Aberdeen will stop now.

"In the event you find it hard to follow this recommendation I need to advise you that you, your wife, and your children will pay a dear price for your refusal to heed this warning. This will be the only call you will receive. Drop all actions concerning Mr. Aberdeen. That is a simple directive and one you should be able to follow.

"In the event you find that hard to do then I would suggest you look at your wife and children and determine how much you're willing to pay to continue the pursuit in trying to find Mr. Aberdeen. Do you have any questions?"

I was standing there holding the phone. I had heard all he had said and it was still working its way into my mind. That damned asshole had just threatened the welfare of my family. I felt my grip on the phone increase as the realization of what he was saying washed over me. "Who the hell are you? If you think for a minute you can call me and make statements like that and threats toward my family you can go to hell."

I was on a roll and started to say more when he interrupted me. "David, you had better control yourself. You are only getting this warning one time. If you continue looking for Mr. Aberdeen there will be a contract issued against your wife and kids.

"David, this is not an idle threat. We have contractors ready to act and once issued it cannot be revoked. For the last time you will stop all actions concerning Aberdeen and you will stop them now and never address the issue again. Good day David."

Just then Helen walked up to me. She could see my face and the fact I was mad as hell. I watched as she stood there looking at me. "David, what is it honey? Is there something wrong?"

I hung up the phone and reached out and took her close to me and stood there holding her. "Honey, there is nothing wrong. It was just some news on the project and it pissed me off, but it will all be worked out in a couple of days."

It was then that I stopped trying to learn anything more about Albert and left it all behind me. It was six months later when I fell into the Time Trap and ended up here. I looked at Paul. "Damn, this was more than just a Time Trap, my supervisor knew there was far more behind Albert's missing and he knew it that day he took me into his office. He knew in some way I was being targeted and I was going to end up in something or someplace like here. The look in his eyes showed me a man who was terrified. I thought it was his being terrified of some power behind him, but now I feel that he was terrified I would figure it out before I was taken.

"Paul, I'm beginning to think that my super knew I was going to be targeted. I'm here because of an overt act by someone or some group. The problem is it was not Albert and if it wasn't, then who were they and what was their purpose? I think Albert brought me here to save me and to stop them.

"As I think about it, my disappearance matches that of Albert's. When he went missing it was sudden and complete. There was no hint, no reason for his disappearing. One moment he was there and the next he was not. And, that matches my coming here to the letter. The only difference is Albert moved before they could.

"I have no doubt Albert is here someplace. I don't know if he is in charge, is being held captive, is planning on an attack on the train, or what. I only know he is here and so am I and that means we are here for the same reason. But the most important thing is Albert brought me here and not the others."

Finally, Lisa came up with the working plan for the next meeting with Albert. "Dad, why can't you play along with him? See if he can determine if you're being deceptive. If he figures you out then you can tell him you were testing him and he just confirmed what you suspected. If he does not challenge you, then in all probability he cannot determine what you're thinking and that gives you the chance to put together a plan and start working on a way to overcome whatever is coming.

"Besides, he has to let you in on something of his plan fairly soon or his need for you will diminish. I would think he needs you badly if he went through all this activity to get you here. If that is the case then I think you have some leverage against him and you should be able to get us some more information on what is going on.

"Once you have then you can come back and we can work something up to counter him or work with him."

"The problem Lisa, is he may not let me come back a second time."

"That could be, but he cannot keep you from waking up. You have to wake up from time to time in order to eat and take care of other personal matters."

She was right, that was my way out and I could use it several times if not whenever I wanted to. "All right, we need to start putting a plan together based on what we know about Albert at this time.

"Now, we know Albert is paranoid and schizophrenic. That means I can question him for more detail as to what he is doing, planning or needing, but I need to take care and make sure I am with him and not opposed to him and what he is doing.

"Next, he is angry and I can use his anger to channel his thoughts into giving me more information about what is behind that anger and his plans for payback.

"We need a better measure on his mental capacity. If he did develop and use the Time Trap to bring me here, then I need to know what else he is capable of.

"In addition, I need to know if his current situation is of his making or if there actually was someone or some group that has kidnapped him and is currently controlling him."

I sat there waiting for any of the others to add to the list, but none did. Paul picked up his notepad and started to write something down and then set it down after he finished. "David, it's important you understand what you are dealing with. Albert is an extremely intelligent person.

"From what I can tell he is way ahead of just about anyone I can think of. Whatever the reason, if I am right, he had progressed to a point his intelligence has actually driven him insane.

"You must be careful in what you say and how you say it. The only thing I can advise you on is you must always remain positive with him and never question what he is doing. By that I mean do not challenge him. If and when you start to ask question, do so in a manner that tells him you are trying to learn. If he challenges you in any way you must remain firm. Do not give in to him. He will do his best to control you and you must let him know or make him understand that will not happen.

"He has a plan and he will work to stay with that plan no matter what. If you do anything that appears to be an attempt to thwart his plan, he will turn on you. Right now, you're his friend and confidant; you want to keep that relationship intact and growing.

"No matter what else happens, you must remain firm in your attitude concerning right and wrong. In his state of mind everything he is doing is right, you must determine in your own mind what is right and what is wrong for you and then hold firm to that belief. He won't like it, but he will respect and accept it.

"Now somewhere along the line you will bc faccd with a judgment call based on your moral standard, not his. When the time comes, he will be measuring you carefully. What you say and do at that time will determine where this whole mess is going. If he determines you're against him then we have failed and the vortex will happen. If he accepts what you have decided, then you will have the opportunity to address the issue and hopefully stop it.

"Now about the environment, you must take a stand right off. Tell him straight out you feel the present environment is not helping you deal with what is happening and you would prefer a more traditional environment. If he expects you to work with him or just consider his situation, you want to do it in a less threatening place sitting face to face as he actually is and not some grotesque appearance. Do you understand me?"

He had said a lot over the last few minutes and I had tried to take it all in. I knew what he was saying and wanting me to do. My problem was I was not sure I could do that. The fact was, I was still catching up with myself as a result of the Time Trap and was not sure I was ready for a mental competition.

I looked at the clock and we had less than an hour to go before he would be coming for me. "Paul, it all still seems to be a dream. The more I think about this mess the more I feel I am not actually here, that this is all a dream or some drug induced hallucination. Having said that, I know I must still function under whatever the circumstances are. I can only tell you I will do my best."

Paul was nodding his head and reached out and patted me on the arm. "David, you'll do just fine. All I can tell you is you need to be the David Albert knows and trusts. Be that David and everything will work out fine. Be firm and refuse anything that goes against that David he knows. He will be measuring everything against that, it is that David he needs and wants."

Pat then got up and walked out the front door and to his car. A few minutes later he returned carrying a small bag in his hand. He walked over to me and placed a bag in my hand and went back and sat down.

I looked at him and then looked down at the bag and opened it. Inside was a coin, an 1881-S Morgan Silver Dollar. I recognized it immediately. It was a coin my father had given to me when I turned twenty-one and I intcndcd to give to Pat when he turned twenty-one. I have no idea how long it had been in the family but that rainbow colored coin brought back a load of memories.

I looked at Pat and placed the coin back into the bag and put the bag in my pocket and smiled and nodded at him. No words were needed.

CHAPTER EIGHT

David Meets Goliath

I was standing in the same medium as before. It was clear like water but I was not sure it was water. From the distance I could see Albert coming toward me, he appeared as he had before. As he approached me, he started to speak when I raised my right hand and asked him to stop. He stopped there in front of me saying nothing, just waiting.

There was no time for formalities I needed to get this going and the first issue was his appearance. I lowered my hand. "Albert I'm here because you want me here but there is a problem, and it's your appearance. I have in my mind that this is not what you actually look like. In fact, I'm certain of it.

"I would prefer you remove this façade and present yourself as you truly are, the Albert I have always known."

He moved to my right and swung around behind me and came up on my left making a complete three hundred sixty degree move around me. He stopped in front of me and then everything started to waver. Slowly at first and then progressively faster the image of him changed. At the same time the water effect went away and in a relatively short time I was standing face to face with Albert.

We were standing in a small room maybe fifteen by twenty feet. It looked more like a den than anything else. In fact, it looked comfortable. The walls were painted a light blue and the ceiling white. There was one door in front of me and it was stained a dark oak color.

There was a couch and a matching chair in one corner and on the opposite side of the room a desk with one chair. Mounted on the wall was a television. I could tell the room was air conditioned. The lighting was subdued but comfortable.

I turned and looked at the rest of the room. I saw a second doorway that led into a kitchenette and next to it was a third door that

165

looked like it led into a bedroom. I would say the area was around eight to nine hundred square feet.

I then turned back to Albert. He had this smile on his face that told me he had enjoyed the entire game and was still in the game playing mode. "Albert, I really don't know what is going on here but I know that you have a greater degree of control over this situation than I or anyone else thinks.

"Albert, you brought me here for a reason and it's time you filled me in on what you are up to and where this meeting is going.

"You are my friend and I tried hard to find you, even to the point of having my life and that of my family threatened. I knew they were using look-a-likes for your public appearances and still I could not find anything else out about you. I think I have a right to know just what the hell happened and what is going on here right this minute."

He walked over to the chair and sat down gesturing me toward the couch. I walked over and sat at the end of the couch closest to him. We sat there for several minute as he thought over my question. "David, it is you, my good friend. These past thirty years have been good to you. How is the family?"

I was stunned by the question he had asked. "Albert what do you mean how is my family? They're all screwed up. Over the past thirty years they have lived with the belief I had ran away and left their mother and them. Helen died about three years ago. I was pulled from my life in 2015 to this place in 2045 and in that time period they have gone through hell. How the hell do you think they are doing?"

I let my feelings go, I wanted him to know this was not a good situation for me and my family. As I spoke, I could see the bewilderment and confusion slide across his face. There was no sign of anger, just the realization things were not as he had thought or planned.

He finally got his composure back. "David, I hadn't thought of that. Don't ask me why because I don't know. I had a need and a purpose in mind when I brought you here and I failed to consider the ramifications of my actions in regards to your life and of your family. Helen has been dead for three years?"

I was nodding my head as he voiced the question. "Yes Albert, she has been dead for three years. In the time frame you have set up that means she lived twenty-seven years after

I disappeared and never knew why I left or where I had gone. I can't imagine the pain and torment that put her through."

By now he was rocking back and forth in his chair holding his hands clasped together between his knees and staring at the floor. Then he looked at me. "I, I don't know what to say. It was never my intentions to cause you or anyone in your family that much trouble.

"Look David, I'm sorry for this and I'll correct that issue right this minute. I'll send you back to your time and deal with this problem on my own. I didn't intend for this to happen; I was just concentrating on what I was doing and not thinking about what it would do to you and Helen. That's terrible."

Right then I knew I had him and I needed to move now. "Albert I'm here and you brought me here. For this time frame the past is set and let's leave it at that. When we're finished here you can return me to my time frame and Helen and I will live our lives as they should be lived.

"Let me show you something." I reached in my pocket and pulled out the small bag and opened it. "Albert this is a coin my father gave me when I turned twenty-one, his father had given it to him when he turned twenty-one. I had planned one day to give this coin to my son when he turned twenty-one and that day I have not yet seen.

"I want that day to come and I want that moment when I give this coin to Pat. Right now, everything I love and lived for is in jeopardy. I am here to address what you are planning and if possible, ensure my family, and their future, is cared for and safe. Do you understand that?"

Albert started to smile and sat back in the chair. "Then you're going to help me?"

"Albert that depends on what it is you want help with and what you want me to do."

He sat there looking at me. I could tell he was measuring everything I was saying. I had an inner feeling that what was coming would be something I didn't want to hear. "David, those people screwed me over in regards to the development of the Super Train. They hauled my ass out of that town and planted me in the middle of this base and have held me here ever since.

"They keep me locked in this room and bring my meals to me. I have spent the past thirty-one years here in these eight hundred square feet. In that time my mind has expanded and grown to a point where I can now control time and space. I know I'm probably insane, that comes with the level of mental development I have achieved.

"I also know with that mental development I can do as I want and when I want. I have demonstrated that with you. That was your first service to me, my being able to bring you forward in time and to this place. I failed to understand that as I did it, I forced your family to live that time frame in real time and they lived with that burden. That's totally unfair and I can assure you when we're done, I will rectify that situation.

"David, I was expecting you to be a whole lot more hostile toward me when we started this meeting. I was going to demonstrate to you what my power really consists of. However, you have thrown me a curve and now I'm not too sure just how we should progress.

"My problem David is my need for revenge is building and this delay is not helping. I need to pay these people back and it's going to start here at this base and you are going to help me. I have not decided as to whether I will set the vortex off or not. Your prior talk has made me think all the innocent

170

do not deserve that ending. But still they aided in this by their inability to act or stand against all the government and those building the Super Train have done.

"Still, their crime is nowhere near that of those who have done this to me. I'm inclined to not destroy the whole world, but I am going to destroy the Super Train and each and every one of those who have put me through this. That David is what you will help me do."

All right, that was his intent, at least we had pulled back from the world but still we had the areas of the country where the tube was being built, we needed to consider. I felt it was time to deal with the rest of Albert's false front. "Albert, I think I can help you, but I still want us to be careful as to any collateral damage that may result. The towns and cities sitting above the tube need to have the same consideration as the rest of the world.

"Second, and possibly most important to me, are you and your current condition. I still have a feeling you are not showing me your true self. If we are going to work together, I need to know who you are Albert, not who you want me to think you are."

171

He again went into a quiet period and sat there looking at the floor. Finally, he looked up at me. "David, I've changed. I didn't want you to see me like I am because it shames me. During my time in isolation, I had nothing to do. They would not give me anything I could use against myself which meant I just sat here looking at the television and watching what they wanted me to watch.

"I began to develop mind exercises and as they developed, I became more and more aware of all there was. My mind started to reach out and delve into whatever it found and in time I was going anywhere I wanted and staying as long as I wanted.

"At first it was all fantasy. But after a time, I started to realize what had been fantasy was becoming more and more real. David, I started to change mentally and then it started to show physically. I was working on my mental activities continuously, almost twenty hours a day.

"That was when the pain started. The whole of my head started to hurt. There was a pressure that kept pressing outward. Maybe three months after the pain and pressures started, I noticed my head seemed to be increasing in size. Without a mirror I couldn't

172

actually see it until one day I looked up at the television. It was off but I could see my reflection. What I saw scared the hell out of me. David, my head had almost doubled in size in a three-month period. I think that's what drove me insane. You realize don't you David I am insane?"

The question punched its way into my mind as I started to nod my head. "Yeah, Albert, I know that. But you're still my friend and that will never end. That's why I came back and that's why I'm willing to help you."

He shook himself and then sat up straight and at that moment I saw a waver or quiver in my view of him and then he changed right there in front of me. He was right, his head had grown. As I sat there looking at him, I noted his head was shaped in an elongation toward the back of his head. It dawned on me I had seen skulls of humans from prehistory digs that were shaped this way.

His head was twice as long as it once had been. His eyes were more deep set and his ears were pulled in deeper into his skull. The mouth and nose were the same as they had always been, well as I remembered them.

173

I reached out and put my hand on the back of his left hand and looked him straight in the eyes. "You are still Albert and I love you."

He sat there looking at me and started to nod his head. "Thank you; I really need that from you. Are you still willing to help me?"

As I sat there, I had the feeling come over me. I might as well have had a sling shot for a weapon when facing the potential of this man's mental powers. I was truly looking at a Goliath and I knew whether I had a sling shot or just my mind I was in deep water.

Scared, hell yes, I was and I think he knew that. I didn't try to hide it. He needed to know I had feelings about this whole mess and I was there under the most unusual of circumstances. Then it came to me. "Albert, do they, the people keeping you here know what you look like and are capable of?"

He started to shake his head. "No, they only see and hear what I want them to see and hear. Right now, I'm being my normal insane self. There is nothing unusual going on in this room.

"You mean they don't know I'm here?"

"That's right. They can only see what I let them see."

"Albert, if you have these abilities then why don't you just stand up and walk out of this place? It would seem to me you could control this entire base without any problem."

He smiled at me and leaned forward. "Because David, I don't want to, at least not right now."

"Then everything going on, with you and this place, is all mental and I'm still lying back at my daughters house sleeping?"

Nodding he replied. "Yes, David that is what is happening right now."

It dawned on me what I was seeing was not necessarily the real situation. This could just as well be a totally mental façade. How the hell do you call an insane man a liar and live to talk about it? "Albert, I am having one hell of a problem and I fear if I ask you it will make you mad and could result in a situation neither one of us wants. But I need to ask, so how am I to know what I am seeing right now is the truth and not just a fabrication like the one you are doing to those holding you?"

He kept that wise knowing it all smile on his face and sat there looking at me. I knew then I was dealing with a man, a being who was by some quirk of nature and time well beyond me in his mental capabilities.

Those who had taken this man and placed him in an isolated environment had created the conditions needed for him to mutate into whatever the hell he was now. I was on a tight rope and he was holding the knife.

"David, I recognize the situation you're in and I understand your fear and worry. Please forgive me for not trusting you completely. I have lived in this situation for all these years and I find I trust no one other than myself.

"David, I know why you're here and I accept that. You are here to try and stop me from carrying out my plan and I accept and understand it. I didn't recognize what I had done to you and Helen and your kids when I pulled you in to my Time Trap, but now that I do, I am taking all into consideration.

"You can stop trying to figure a way to divert or stop my taking revenge. It is going to happen; the only issue is the means I take to achieve my revenge. You helped me recognize I was too fixated on my target and forgot about all the innocent would pay for their meanness and greed. I have altered my plans as a result.

"The issue now is to locate those I am targeting and bring all of them to judgment, a judgment I plan to be unique for each and every one of them. David, I can and will take my revenge against them. The fact is David, I no longer need you. You have fulfilled my need by being my conscience and that has made all the difference in the world.

"I have considered sending you back but have decided I will keep you here for the time being and I may well need you again to finish things up."

Just then he stopped and looked at me, his face getting redder and redder. His eyes opened even wider and he sat up straight. He just exploded in front of me. His mouth opened and the most terrifying scream came out of him. I didn't know what the hell was going on but he was mad, so mad I knew he could kill.

"David, don't you ever try to work me again." He screamed. "Never will you try to do that again. I love you David, but I will kill you if you try that again."

I was dumb founded. I had no idea what I had just done or maybe thought but whatever it was it set him off. Out of nowhere he had slid into a temper explosion the likes of which I had never seen or experienced.

Just as fast as it started it stopped. He sat there looking at me. Myself? I was blasted. I had no idea as to what had just happened. I'm sure I was white as a sheet and scared half to death. The fact was I wanted to throw up.

We sat there for several minutes. "David, I know your mind. I have just finished scanning it in total and I found the actions you were considering against me. Those I will not tolerate. You are my friend and I love you. I know why you're trying to stop me and I understand and have altered my plans as a result.

"I recognized just what I have done to you and for that I am sorry, but that does not mean I will sit here and let you kill my plans. I have spent over thirty years planning this action and no one, not even you, are going to stop me.

"However, you need to know the vortex is still a consideration. I have not ruled it out completely. It just may be this world needs to be destroyed and a new beginning started just like Noah and the flood."

Oh my God, he has developed a God image. As soon as that thought hit me, he smiled at me and raised his right hand pointing his index finger at me. "Now David, that's not a good thought you just had."

That did it. It was my time to explode and I did just that. I stood up and stomped out into the middle of the room and then turned facing Albert. "What the hell do you expect me to do? Just because of all the shit those people have dumped on you, you feel you have a right of retribution and I don't argue with. But damn it anyway, I didn't deserve being pulled thirty years into the future only to leave my wife and kids behind wondering what the hell happened to their father and her husband.

"I missed twenty-seven years of being with my wife and then she died without me still not knowing what happened to me. I don't care if you're going to send me back, she still had to live through that experience and for that there is no excuse and no reasoning that can justify it.

"You have decided you deserve to pay the world back for what happened to you, well just when the hell do, we get to pay you back for what you have done to us. When the hell did God give you the all-mighty right to judge the entire world because of what

179

happened to you and your mistreatment by those bastards.

"So far in this whole damn mess I have gotten it from the company, the people they hired to threaten me and my family and now you. I'm to the point where I wished I had never heard of the Super Train. As a matter of fact, I am just about to the point where I wished I have never heard of you. Understand?"

I had been stomping around the room waving my hand and letting everything go. I didn't know just what I was saying, I just let things fly. I was so mad if I ever cooled down, I would probably be killed on the spot by Albert. This was the end and I didn't care what Albert or anyone else thought for that matter. It was a case of screw them all, just get it over with.

I finally stopped moving and stood there; sweat pouring off my face and down my neck. I had lost it and I knew it and all I could do was stand there and wait for it to hit me. It was dead silent. I was breathing like I had just run the mile and I was shaking all over.

I looked over at Albert and he was sitting there looking at me. The expression on his face was one of bewilderment and shock. His mouth was open and he wasn't moving, just sitting there looking at me.

Finally, he stood and walked over to me and put his arms around me and pulled me close to him. We stayed that way for several minutes and then I reached up and took hold of him. We both started to cry and I knew it was genuine and from deep inside for both of us.

We moved back to the couch and sat down side by side. "Albert, we need to end this and end it now. If you're going to take retribution against those who did this to you then do it now and get it over with. No more games, no more playing around, just step out and get it over with.

"Albert, you know what you want to do here other than to demonstrate your abilities and I recognize those as well. It was thirty years ago when a group of men made the determination to let you design their project and then they set out on a plan to control you first and then control the use of that power plant.

"In doing that they violated every fundamental concept of right and justice and they destroyed your life. That is reprehensible

181

and frankly they deserve anything that happens to them. But, the rest of the world does not. The rest of us are just as much victims of that group as you have been and currently are.

"Albert, if you are going to take action then do so now, targeting those who are responsible for this act. I would have no problem if you could go back and completely and totally take the Super Train out of existence. Erase it from all time and memory and the world would be better off without it.

"But, Albert, if one innocent person falls because of your actions against those who have done this to you, I'm telling you here and now I will never consider you a friend and brother again.

I hate even the thought of that, but that is how I feel and if it means my death then so be it, right now I don't have Helen so what the hell is life worth to me anyway?"

He reached over and put his right hand on my left knee and started to nod his head. "All right David, I understand what you're saying. It hurts but I realize now just how out of line I have been. I'm not so insane I don't see what I have done and I didn't realize how it has hurt those who are close to me. That was never intended to happen, but it did and for that I am truly sorry.

"I agree, I need to get off my high horse and do what needs to be done. David, I have decided not to use the vortex but the plan I have still involves you and it involves you in 2015 not here in 2045. Do you understand?"

Now we were getting down to something more reasonable. "No Albert, I don't, but I'm willing to listen and if it sounds reasonable then I willing to go for it."

He repositioned himself on the couch and started in. "David, I have decided I want to eliminate the Super Train all together. I feel the best way to do is to kill it at the beginning, before it gets a chance to be built. The best place for that is during the design stage. David, I'm looking at a faulty design layout."

"All right Albert, but how are we going to do that?"

"We'll do it through my design calculations. I created that beast and I am the only one who knows how the design works and what brought it together. If we kill it at that point there is no one who can step in and replace me."

Yeah, I could see where he was coming from but there was a problem. "Albert, does all this moving around in time create any kind of a situation where someone may know or remember you had actually and successfully designed and built that machine?"

"No David, we will go far enough into the past to make the initial change. No one will know anything about the concept or science behind it. It will be just an unsolvable problem we would face."

"Good, I can see that but that brings up another issue. If the change is made then the company will never take you or kidnap you and they will in turn have no idea as to what your actions against them are for. Albert, they would be innocent victims."

An even stranger look came across his face. "Oh, that wouldn't do any good. You're right I wouldn't have anyone to take revenge on." He looked at me. "David, that won't work, that won't work at all."

I couldn't help it, I started to laugh. Within seconds he was laughing as well and we let it all out. Finally, after several minutes I reached over and grabbed his arm. "How about this Albert, what do you think about taking your revenge now against those people and then moving back in time to the initial design stage of the machine and eliminating the formulas and design elements you have been talking about?

"At the same time, you can drop me off in 2015 on that June day and I can continue to live my life with my wife and family."

He stood up and started walking around the room and then looked over at me. "I think we can do that. It will take some planning but I think it is workable. That way I can eliminate the machine and deal with those people and even move back to the time before they took me and live my life as it should have been lived."

Oh, this was going to be a complex plan if ever I saw one. He was going to get the guys who had done this to him, then go back in time to the design phase of the Super Train and kill the power plant. During the process he was going to drop me off at my originating time in 2015 and then last of all insert himself back into his life at that point before they kidnapped him.

He was walking around ringing his hands and talking to himself as he developed his plan. It was then he turned to me. "David, I don't need you anymore. At least not for a while so why don't you go back to your kids and layout what is going to happen. When I'm ready I'll call you back. Is that all right?"

This was the first time he was thinking in a rational manner. "Why yes Albert, that would work just fine, you're sure you don't need me?"

"No, I don't think so, but if I do, I'll call you back."

"That works for me, Albert. How long do you think it will be before you're ready to call me back?"

"Not long David, I think I'll have everything ready in about three to four days. Oh, David thanks, you've helped more than you could ever imagine."

It then came to me. "Albert, if you change the design of the power plant before they took you, won't that change the future for all of us?"

"Yeah, I've thought about that and I think I can work that out. The design issue will be of such it won't come up before that day in June when I took you. Everything will remain the same up till that point. In fact, they will kidnap me and when the design fails, they will release me and everything will work into its rightful place."

He was thinking now and he would not miss anything. The mind they forced him to develop will do its job and then revert back to the old Albert when he initiates his plan. There was still a long way to go, but there was an end in sight and it looked good from my point of view.

I gave the signal to Paul and after a few minutes I woke up. All four were standing there looking at me. Paul leaned over. "Well, what happened?"

Who could blame them; I had been gone for several hours to them and only minutes for me? I sat up and shook my head. "All right, here it is in a nutshell. Albert has pulled away from the vortex issue and is concentrating on taking his revenge out on those who did this to him. He is currently working up a plan to change the design of the power plant at the point in time before he was kidnapped.

"The design change will affect the power plant at a point after the day of my disappearance. In that way I can return to the exact time when I disappeared and return home as if nothing happened.

187

"Albert will still be kidnapped but upon the failure of his design they will release him and he will live his normal life.

"It's a complex plan and may take him three or four days to complete. When he is ready, he will call me back and we will then go over the plan and if it is what I think it will be then he will implement it. That means we will all go back to our normal lives and I will return home and Helen and I will live for twenty-seven years before she dies and you kids will have us both during that time."

Lisa, as usual, came up with the big question. "Dad, what about your memory, will you remember all this or will it be as it was on that day and minute when you disappeared?"

I didn't have an answer for that but I had an idea. "Lisa, I'm not sure just what will happen but if it works as I understand it, I will remember nothing of the jump, and being here with you. I will return home from the post office on time and ready to go out and mow the lawn. That's the best I can do for you."

She was nodding her head and smiling at me. She knew she was having a special time and when I returned to my time the continuum would change for us all and we would be as it should have been, living our lives from 2015 on with the future unknown.

I couldn't help it; there we were in this amazing situation and I was now starting to think about the science and reality behind all that had happened. Time, as it turns out, is a strange and flexible dimension. In the past we thought time was set and when time ran nothing changed it.

As our understanding of time progressed, we determined that time for one person was not the same for another. That time in one place was different from time in another place. The amount of difference may not be that much, but the point is time is different for each of us in relationship to where we're at. Time is not the marching and never-ending advancement of space. It flows and ebbs with the dynamics of space and all the influences that exist here.

Time is an enigma, a mystery mankind has been trying to deal with since the first man looked at the sun and recognized as it moved, so passed his days and nights and his life. Time is complex and if and when mankind unlocks the mysteries of time, he will discover a realm so far beyond his imagination he will surely question his sanity.

189

Albert's actions to date have created more problems in the time continuum for me and my kids and I really did not think he could straighten it out. I sure as hell hoped he could. Well, I guess the old adage really applies here, 'time will tell'.

CHAPTER NINE

The Puzzle of Time

We had spent the entire day and late into the night before we finally called it quits. Pat and his wife went home and Lisa and I remained for a time to visit with Jane. The professor left at the same time Pat left. We had all agreed to meet the next time Albert contacted me.

Lisa, Jane and I were sitting there looking at one another when Jane finally spoke. "Dad, I hope you understand how I felt when I first met you. I couldn't believe you had come back after leaving us so suddenly thirty years ago. That has haunted me all my life and I guess I was holding a lot of hate for you and what you did to mom."

As I listened to her, I could see she was dealing with a whole lot of guilt and she needed to be assured she was all right and I held nothing against her. "Jane, you were at a young age and frankly the most vulnerable of the three of you. I understand the hurt and pain you went through. Hon, we never know what will happen in our lives and we surely don't need anyone playing around with our time continuums.

"Albert did and when he did it fouled everything up for the four of us. When I told him about it, he was as surprised as the rest of us and felt terrible. He said, and I believe him, he never intended to do that to us but he would make sure when he returned me, he would be sure to set me back at the exact time and place I left.

"Jane, when this is over you will remember nothing of it. You will live with your family, your brother, sister, mother and father just as it had always been. When 2045 comes around you will know nothing of this happening here in this time continuum. It will have never existed from your view point.

"Right now, that's the plan and if I can't do anything about it, that's the way it will end. I fully plan on spending the rest of Helens life with her. I have faith it will happen and my life will be restored to the second in time when it was uprooted.

"Yes, there is the chance it will go wrong and I will not make it back to my time and place. If that happens then I don't know what to say. I pray I will not survive it. My most urgent concern is for you kids. If nothing else works out I need to have you find a solution to your wanting to know where I went. If I'm killed then I want that fact related to each of you so you can live your lives knowing what happened and not facing a mystery the rest of your lives."

The two girls sat there and finally Lisa stood up. "Well, I think this day has gone on just about long enough so I would suggest dad and I head for home and some much-needed sleep."

We got up and I gave Jane a kiss on the cheek and we left. As before it was thirty minutes back to Lisa's place and when we got inside, I had that feeling come over me maybe I didn't want to go to sleep. I quickly pushed that aside. Albert had said it would be several days before he would need me and I could probably not worry about being disturbed anytime soon.

As it turned out I slept the night through without the slightest hint of Albert being present. I woke the next morning refreshed and eager to see the new day. Lisa was getting ready for work as I entered the kitchen. "Dad, will you be all right here by yourself today? I simply have to make a showing at the office today. I may not have to stay the whole day."

"I'll be just fine. You go and stay all day if need be, I'm just going to sit back and relax and then probably do some thinking on what I have seen and learned so far and what I expect will come by the end of the week."

She finished making her lunch, got her coat and came over to me and gave me a hug and kiss. "I'll see you at five."

I nodded and hugged her back. "Now, you don't worry about me, I have more than enough to keep me busy. If it will make you feel better you can call and check up on me every few hours. I'm not leaving this house; it's just not smart at this time."

I watched as she backed out of the driveway and headed up the street. I got a cup of coffee, took a roll out of the bread box and sat down at the table and started to read the paper. As I started to read it was just an ordinary paper but then something started to happen. Right in front of me the titles and headlines started to change. I sat there watching the progression of the headlines and then realized things were in reverse. That is, the headlines were going back in time. I dropped the paper and it all stopped.

What the hell, I knew my watch would act up if I took it off but the newspaper actually changing in my hand as I held it. There was only one explanation and that was the fact I was not synchronized with the current time and place. I was still in 2015 and I was being reminded of it.

Then it hit me, let the paper go back and watch the progression of the headlines and see what came up. The front page was national and international news and was perfect. I got up and got a pad and sat down and picked the paper up again. It had returned to today's headlines and then it started to go in reverse. I read each headline and found I could slow and stop the progression as I wanted.

It wasn't long before I came to the first headline that meant something. It was about the coming test of the new Super Train and the target of the test was to run from New

York to Bradford, Pennsylvania a distance of two hundred fifty miles give or take a few miles.

That had to be Albert's target he had set at first. I was not sure if he was still going to target the train. If he kept his word, he was going to deal with the train back in 2014 so this train test should run as scheduled.

It dawned on me he had targeted the train test for the vortex and if he was going to keep his word that was now off and the test should go as scheduled. I looked for a date of the test and there it was July 1, 2045.

If I remember right, he brought me here on June 6, 2045 so that means the test is still three weeks away. It would still be an attractive target for Albert and I made a mental note to make sure he did not change his mind on that issue.

I picked up the paper and the dates started to move backward again. The next headline that registered to me was the announcement of a coming progress report meeting on the Super Train. The report stated the president and chairman of the company who was building Super Train would be there personally to make the report. It also mentioned Albert Aberdeen would be there to

196

answer questions on the progress of the system.

For some reason the headline seemed to be important, could it be it was that meeting Albert planned to take his revenge on those who kidnapped and mistreated him? That would be logical but what about his plan to go back and change the formulas in the plans. If he did then this meeting and the test in the prior headline would not even be in the paper.

I sat there watching the paper and headline announcing this coming meeting when the text of the article changed. At first, I thought it had just shifted but no it had changed right there in front of my eyes.

A shot of fear charged through my mind as the realization Albert had done something to change this article right there in front of me. I reread the article and it was now an announcement of the coming meeting had been cancelled with no reason given.

I set the paper down and watched for the prior article on the coming Super Train test to come back. There it was and the headline had changed as well. "Super Train preliminary testing failed."

Just what had Albert done, I had no idea but he was up to something and I had thought he was going to wait until he had me come back to meet with him. I decided to read the article in full. As I started it was clear what had happened was unexpected to the reporter and those he had been interviewing.

It seems the main power plant in the engine had failed a test. That test had to do with the primary power production module that controlled the conduction turbines of the system. The engine could run at its preliminary startup phase, but when they attempted to shift into the primary power production system it crashed.

It not only crashed it crashed and burned. The entire interior of the main engine went up in flames. No one lost their life when the incident happened, but the power plant was a total loss. Any and all testing of the system and the train would be indefinitely postponed.

He couldn't have, no he wouldn't have gone back to 2014 already and made the changes in the design of the power plant. He planned on taking me back with him.

I felt a surge of fear go through me. Was he leaving me here and not planning on taking me back or sending me back? I had no idea as to what the hell was going on but something big had happened and I was completely in the dark about it.

It was then when he touched me. "David, it's alright. I've changed my plans and I have taken the action against the system early. I left you out because I did not want to jeopardize your return or your welfare. All you need to know right now is the system has been killed and I did it without hurting one single person.

"I have other actions I need to take and when I complete those, I will deal with you and your family situation. I just want you to know you will be returned and all this will change when you continue on home from the post office in 2015.

"Trust me David, you helped me get things straight in my mind and I am now making my move on that damn thing and those who killed my life. All you need to do is watch the headlines and it will all become clear. In four days, I will bring you to me and will lay it all out and start the process of sending you home."

I was at a loss as to what to do. I could say nothing and I could do nothing. He had made his plans and they were way ahead of me. The Super Train was dead and next would come those who had tormented him. I had a deep-down feeling thing were going to get really bad in a short time. Maybe it was better I and my family were out of this.

I spent the rest of the day sitting there at the table looking at the newspaper headlines go by. It was late afternoon, about four o'clock, when I saw the first meaningful headline. "Police and family still baffled by the disappearance of husband and father."

I had to read the report. It was about the disappearance of Mr. David Jacobs and his car still haunted the police? "It has been seven months since David Jacobs dropped out of sight. In that time the police have found absolutely nothing on where he went or what happened to him and his car.

"The search for Jacobs has expanded across the state and the eastern region of the nation and still there is nothing. There has been no use of any credit cards, gas card, or checks as of now. Police Captain Taylor stated it was as if he just vanished into thin air. There's nothing. It's almost as if Mr. Jacobs never existed in the first place. We know that's not true but that's how it reads.

"When contacted, Mrs. Jacobs could only say her husband had gone to the post office and that's the last she saw of him. They had learned Mr. Jacobs had gotten to the post office and mailed the items he was going there for. All items reached their destination. There have been no new leads as to where he could have gone or if he has been in contact with anyone.

"Further contacts with the police have resulted in no new information. They did say the search had been expanded to a nationwide search which was started a week after he disappeared and still there have been no reports of sightings."

I put my hand on the paper again and it continued back in time until it hit June 6, 2015 and stopped there. I had gone back thirty years in the paper and now felt I wanted to let it start back toward 2045.

I pushed the paper back to the middle of the table and it started to move forward in time. I found as it speeded up, I could place my hand close to the paper and it would slow it down. So, I sat there watching time move along as the headlines changed from day to day.

The paper had moved ahead when I saw a smaller headline at the bottom of the page. I placed my hand on the paper and it stopped moving in time. The head line read. "Other missing member of the Super Train development team still missing."

I felt a cold chill run up my back as I realized someone had tied the missing of Albert to my disappearance. I read on. "Albert Aberdeen had been reported missing in 2014. Research conducted by this paper had found Mr. Aberdeen was a team member with Mr. David Jacobs who disappeared about eight months ago.

"No information on the whereabouts of Mr. Aberdeen had come up till right now. While contacting the company Aberdeen and Jacobs works for, they advised Mr. Aberdeen had been assigned to a top-secret project and he was not available for interviews. He would be present at a coming conference on the development of the Super Train.

"The company advised Mr. Aberdeen's situation was one of national importance and once his assignment on part of the Super Train had been completed, he was no longer restricted. There was no explanation as to what restricted meant.

"Mr. Aberdeen was present at the conference and made a presentation on the progression of the Super Train and the time line was being developed for its initial testing. At that time the media had its first opportunity to ask questions of Mr. Aberdeen about the project."

I knew this was the first time they had slipped the look-a-like in to act as Albert. There had to be another article further along that will cover the conference and the Aberdeen interview.

I let the paper start moving ahead again and after three weeks there it was. A minor headline situated at the bottom of the page. "Aberdeen Advises He Finished Project"

As I read on, it was clear this was not Albert, the terminology he used was not the same. Yet it made little or no difference, those people did not know him and probably had never seen him before this meeting.

The report continued and was actually rather generic in nature. He had been pulled from the primary team and assigned to a select team to deal with a specific issue in the overall design of the train. Once finished and proven successful he would then be reassigned back to his primary job duties.

What a line of crap that was. Yet, I had not been there and so how could I doubt what was being said, other than I knew the one they interviewed was not Albert.

It was clear they intended never to let Albert go and he would sit there in that room and slowly mutate into what he was at this time in 2045. They had no idea as to what they had created, but they were about to learn, the hard way.

CHAPTER TEN

Time to Take His Revenge

I let the paper move ahead and then I saw the next big issue headline. "Staff Supervisor of Super Train Found Dead"

The headline appeared twenty-seven years into the disappearance of Albert, just three years back from me here and now. "Mr. Robert Stanly was found by staff personnel this morning in the main design facilities for the Super Train. He had been crushed by an elevator. It appeared as he entered the elevator its braking system had failed and it dropped just as he was stepping into it. He was killed instantly."

Albert was starting at the lowest level of responsibility and he was going to work his way up to the top executives. I doubted very much it was instantly. Knowing Albert, it was methodical and step by step.

…"Hey Stan, the gang is going over to Bruno's for a couple of beers, you coming?"

"Yeah Larry, I have a couple of things to clear up and I'll be right over. Save me a place."

"Will do Stan, see you in a few."

"All right I have the schedule completed for the interview tomorrow. Everyone has been notified and Albert's double is already in town. I just need to let the boss know it's all set and I can cut out for the day."

"Yes, Mr. Longley, I have the scheduling completed and all the media people have been advised. Everything's a go sir."

"Good work Stan. You'll be there when this thing kicks off?"

"Yes sir. I should be there before you and the others get there. Is there anything special you'll need?"

"No Stan, I think you have it all covered. You understand the importance of this appearance, don't you?"

"Yes, sir I do, things will go off like clockwork. I can't think of anything we have not covered."

"All right Stan, we'll see you tomorrow at ten."

"Yes Sir Mr. Longley."

"That's it and it's time to celebrate."

"You really don't want to celebrate Stan."

"What, who is that?"

"Stan, I said you really don't want to celebrate. Just what the hell do you have to celebrate anyway?"

"Who are you and where are you?"

"Stan, you're not listening to me, you know who I am."

He stood there looking around him. He was not hallucinating; he had heard a voice and it sounded familiar to him. But he couldn't put a finger on just who the hell it was.

"Come on Stan, you're not applying yourself. You know who I am; you're just not trying hard enough. Now think about it and try again."

"No, it couldn't, be you?"

"You're almost there Stan; just push it a little further."

"Albert, is that you?"

"Good for you Stan, now we're moving along. Yes, it's me, and you and I have a couple of issues to deal with and settle this evening."

"Albert, I think you had better come out and face me head on. How the hell did you get out of the base anyway?"

"Oh Stan, you have no idea what is going on here, but you're about to find out shortly. You were one of those who set me up for the kidnapping and you're about to pay for it."

"Wait a minute Albert. I only did what I was told to do. You may not know it but I was threatened as well, if I failed to assist in your kidnapping. Albert, I had no choice."

"Yes Stan, you had a choice and you choose yourself. That was a conscious decision by you and it means you selected to sacrifice me for your own gain. That Stan was your greatest mistake."

"Look Albert, you can't hold me responsible for what others planned and did. I told them I didn't like what they were doing, but I was told it was either you or me and I had to protect myself. Hell, I have a family to care for. What did you expect me to do?"

"The right thing Stan, the right thing and you didn't."

"Albert, what the hell are you doing? Let go of me, let go of me now."

Just then the elevator door opened and Stan found he was being pushed toward to open doors.

"Albert please, I didn't have a choice. If I fought them, they would have killed me. Albert, I was fighting for my life."

As he approached the elevator, he noticed the car started to slide down even with the doors standing open. It was then he realized what was going to happen if he didn't break loose and get away.

He started to fight with everything he had, but how do you fight something you can't see. How do you fight something that is so powerful you can't resist any of its actions?

"For God sakes Albert, you can't do this. Listen to me, they made me. I had no control. Damn-it Albert, stop."…

I sat there looking at the article knowing full well his revenge had started and it wouldn't stop until Albert had taken his last pint of blood. I had no idea as to how many were to die, but I was sure if it started with a staff supervisor then it meant there was a rather long list of those, he planned on dealing with.

I pulled my hand back from the paper and let the headline start to roll again. In less than a week the next headline appeared. "Security Comptroller of the Super Train Project Found Dead"

I started to scan the article and found a Levi Danials had been killed by electrocution while checking out a security panel in the main control building. He had been by himself and had apparently opened the back of a panel for some reason and was found lying at the panel door with his hand jammed into a six-hundred-amp breaker.

…"Yes Howard, you can go, I have the main system on line and the walking patrols are on post. I have a number of reports I need to finish before I leave."

"All right boss, I'll see you in the morning. By the way, what's the plan for tomorrow?"

"Actually Howard, we have little to do. The public news conference is the only thing on the agenda and the traveling security units have that one covered. Everything here at the base is taken care of."

"All right boss, See you tomorrow."

"Fine Howard, see you in the morning."

Levi continued setting up the display for the coming meetings when he had this strange feeling come over him. It was like someone had just entered the room. He stood there looking around and then shrugged his shoulders and returned to his project in preparing for the staff meeting in the morning.

He couldn't overcome that feeling someone was watching him. Not only was someone watching him, but whoever was watching him was right there in the room with him. He stopped and remained still and then started to look around, nothing.

He tried to shrug it off again but the more he tried to avoid it the more intense the feeling became. It was then he heard it. Just a whisper of a sound and it was all around him. Then it was a word, a single word he could now hear, "Traitor."

"Who's there? Who are you?"

Nothing, it felt like something was there right next to him, but there was no response. He didn't like the feeling he was experiencing and decided to leave and come in early in the morning to finish the prep work.

He went to his office to get his jacket and belongings. When he entered the office and walked across to his chair where his jacket was hanging, the door slowly closed and he heard the locking mechanism fall into place.

Levi froze, looking around the room for something that wasn't there. He then heard it again, "Traitor."

"All right, enough with the games. Who's doing this and I want to know right now?"

"Levi Danials, you took the wrong side when you turned on me. You chose your side and now you're going to learn it was a bad choice is as good as a death sentence."

"Who the hell is here? Who are you and where are you?"

"Levi, I'm right in front of you. Open your eyes and you will see me. Come on open your eyes and look for me, I'm standing right here looking at you."

He concentrated on the other side of the desk and then he saw it. A faint outline of a human body, but he could not tell who or what it was. "Concentrate Levi you're starting to see me and all you need do is work a little harder and everything will become clear to you."

As the figure increased in clarity, he started to recognize the shape and posture of the being there in front of him. "Albert, is that you?"

"Good for you Levi, you are doing great. Yes, it's me and you're about to see just what you have done to me and what you are going to pay for."

Levi stood there as the figure became more and more visible. Oh, it was Albert alright but not the Albert he had remembered or expected. The body was what Albert had looked like, but the head was something entirely different. In a word it was grotesque. Levi's reaction was one of fear and then terror as he began to recognize the magnitude of the situation.

"Levi, you turned on me when they came for me and for that you will pay. Today I take my revenge on all those who took my life from me and sent me to this condition. Today all debts will be collected and all judgments carried out. Today Levi you shall die for your treachery."

"Come on Albert, you can't be serious. I didn't do anything to you. Yes, I was here and present when they came and got you but beyond that I did nothing against you."

"That my dear Levi is wrong. The fact is you stood there and witnessed what they did to me and then remained silent, taking no action to try and stop or support me. You gave me up to them Levi and for that I hold you responsible for the traitor you are. For that you will die."

"Albert, you can't be serious. They made me cooperate or they would have killed me. It was either you or me and I had no choice, it had to be you. Albert, you would have been taken whether I tried to stop them or not."

"No Levi, you physically helped them. Don't try to hide it from me. I know what you did and you know as well. You called and advised them when everyone else was gone and I was there alone in the office. You then left the office and walked down the hall and waited until they left with me all bound up."

At first, he was not sure anything was happening and then he felt the pressure on his chest. It was like the grasp of a child holding on tight and then it increased and in minutes it was like a bear was crushing him. It spread all over his body and he was finding he could no longer talk. All that came out was a groan and the more he let out the less air he could draw back in.

His hands gripped the back of the chair as the pressure increased. His body went stiff and he could no longer even give out a groan as the life was being squeezed out of him. The last thing he saw was Albert standing there with a smile on his face.

His body then floated through the office door and down the hall to the Security section and then in to the main control room where all the high-powered panels were located. His body was lowered to the floor and then slid behind one of the main power panels."...

The headlines were changing at a regular rate by this time. The police had found the two bodies and were at a loss as to what or how these two men had died. One thing they knew was both had died in the most agonizing way possible. One of the lead investigators had made a comment to the media he expected the deaths to continue until they found whoever was doing this.

A week passed and a name I knew well appeared in the headlines. Frank Wilkerson, Vice Chairman of the Grand Futures INC. had been found dead in his swimming pool that morning by staff personnel at his residence.

…"Thanks Jay, you said they still had no answers as to how Stan and now Levi died?"

"That's right Frank; they found him in the security power facility this morning. Frank, he had had every bone in his body broken and all the organs in his body had been pushed and mashed together."

"Any lead as to who did this?"

"Nothing Frank, all they can say is whoever killed him, killed him in a way no one can relate to. Frank, the man was crushed together and left in a pile on the floor with his face looking straight up at the ceiling."

Frank hung up the phone and sat there looking out the front window of his home. He was a single man living in a home made up of 46 rooms with a garage that could house all the cars in the local police department. He also had a house staff of six who tended to all his needs.

He sat there thinking about the two men who had been killed. He knew both men and had worked with them in the past, the most recent being the Albert Aberdeen incident. As he sat there, he started to tie the two issues together. Both men had been involved in Albert's abduction and now both men were dead. A chill ran up his back as he continued to tie events together.

"You have it figured out, don't you Frank?"

The voice scared the hell out of him as he jumped to his feet and looked around. "Who's there?"

"Frank, you know who it is. Why in the last five minutes you have tied it all together, so guess again and I bet you'll get it right."

"Albert, is that you?"

"Good job Frank, of course it's me. Who else would come here to your home in this way?"

Frank was looking around the room trying to determine just where the voice was coming from. He had a .45 in the desk just on the other side of the room and if he could get there and get that gun and determine where Albert was, he would end this thing now.

Just then he heard the desk drawer open and when he looked over at the desk, he saw the gun coming up out of the drawer. "Frank, this is what you wanted isn't it. Now the thought you wanted to get this gun and use it on me makes me a little mad, but I'll set that aside for now.

"Right now, we need to talk and I think you had better sit down and listen to me very carefully. I have a few things we need to address before I finish up here."

"Albert, you had better start to think about what you're doing. You may think you have control of this situation, but I can assure you, you're wrong. In the end Albert, you cannot survive without the company. We have control over every aspect of your life. That means if we stop providing for you then you cannot survive."

"That's thought-provoking Frank, but I'm afraid you have it all wrong. Frank, I have already killed the Super Train. It will never be successful and every cent you have spent on it is gone. Next, I have a list of people I am now dealing with and I'm afraid you are number three on that list. Tonight, you face judgment for all you've done over the years. All the

218

people you have walked on or destroyed during that time.

"No, Frank your time has come and as a result I have decided it will be slow and painful. I want you to feel every year you have taken from my life and the lives of everyone else you have mistreated. Frank, I have something special waiting for you. I really hope you appreciate the uniqueness and time it took for me to work this up."

"I think it's time for you to leave Albert. Right now, a team of men are entering your apartment and will deal with you as you should have been years ago. When I first heard your voice, I activated a response alarm and you should be feeling the first round hitting you any second."

He stood there waiting and heard nothing from Albert. A smile crossed his face as he walked over to the chair he had been sitting in and sat down, picking up the book he had been reading.

The first round hit him in the left shoulder passing through and hitting the wall across from his chair. The level of fear charging across his brain ripped into him as he screamed in agony.

"Frank, they came and they died just as fast. The entire base is now under my control. Every person at that base is now dead and no one can gain entry into it.

"You missed it Frank. You thought you had total control of me, but you forgot my brain. The one thing you wanted the most you left intact and it is my brain that is now controlling all you know or thought you knew.

"You lousy excuse for a human being, you're going to pay for all you have done to me in these past years. You're going to pay for the life, my life, you destroyed and you will pay like no man has ever paid before.

"When I'm done with you everyone that sees or hears of your death will shake in fear knowing full well, I am still alive and capable of unspeakable acts against those who have wronged me."

Frank sat there with his eyes closed waiting for Albert to finish his tirade. Once Albert stopped, Frank opened his eyes. "Albert, you're sick as hell. If you think you can outsmart the combined minds of the entire company, you're badly mistaken. Albert, we made you and we can end you just as fast.

Now you have had your time with the other two and we'll let that go.

You will return to your apartment and release the base to our people and we will see you are taken care of for the rest of your life. Albert, it's either that or we'll kill you here and now."

The second round came in and hit his left knee cap. The pain hit his mind and he collapsed in agony. "Stop it, stop it right now. You damn fool; you're killing your only chance of living a reasonably well life. We'll take care of you and you will have anything you want."

The third round hit his right knee causing him to thrash around in the chair falling out and onto the floor. The fourth round hit his right shoulder punching though and into the floor. By this time blood was flowing freely from his four wounds when the fifth one hit.

The round tore through his right wrist destroying his use of that hand. By now he was no longer screaming but moaning and laying there, his mind in a state of complete confusion and unable to think.

It was then he saw the form of a person standing over him. Slowly it formed and became solid right there in front of him. His eyes were drawn to the head, a head he had never seen before.

He closed his eyes wanting the vision of that head to leave his mind and when he looked again it was the same. "Albert, that can't, be you? What happened, what went wrong?"

Albert leaned down and over him. "That Frank is what you made of me. You locked me in a room and left me there, eventually forgetting all about me. Well, I never forgot about you. The more I thought the more my mind mutated and the greater my mental capacity increased.

"Frank, I know what you did, what you're doing and what you are planning on doing. You made me Frank and now I'm coming back to make you pay.

"You locked me away and then forgot about me and then this happened and once that took place you were doomed. Now Frank, you are going to pay and every one of those who were involved will have their time as well."

Frank lay there watching Albert move around him. He knew Albert was insane and nothing he could say or do would change his mind.

The next round tore through his left wrist. He tried to respond but there was nothing there. After being hit with six .45 caliber rounds, he could no longer feel the additional pain.

He opened his eyes again seeing the gun moving over the desk and settling on the desk out of his sight. Then he heard the door to his den open onto the veranda. He felt his body being dragged across the floor and through the door and out to the pool.

As he laid there, he was looking at the pool he knew was where, it was going to come to an end. "Albert please, you have to listen to me. What you're doing is wrong and will solve nothing. It will do you no good to kill me. Do you understand?

"Albert, if you kill me, I can do nothing to help you, I'm your only source of relief. Albert, listen to me, you can't do this it's all wrong."

"Frank, I have listened to three of you now and you all have the same thing to say. I'm wrong. I can't do this. You had nothing to do with this situation.

"Every one of you has denied your culpability in my situation. You have all claimed your innocence. The problem with that Frank is you're not innocent. The fact is Frank, you're one of the primary movers in the destruction of my life and now you're about to pay for it."

Frank felt himself sliding across the veranda toward the pool. He couldn't move or stop the slide to his death."…

I sat there looking at the headline knowing full well the terror that was developing across the whole of the Super Train organization was real. There was a purge taking place and no one could stop it or change the final outcome.

Albert had figured a way to take his payback and do it in a manner that would tell the world of his pain and hate. The bottom line was the world was not paying for it. At least not yet, I knew then and there the battle was not over, Albert could still take his final action and move directed on the world.

CHAPTER ELEVEN

The Retribution Continues

…Theodor Banister had just finished with a briefing on the tragic events in the death of three of the company's top managers. His Security Director, Delbert Kingsly was sure the deaths were all tied together and others within the management team were at risk.

The briefing had included the plan to increase the security coverage of all the companies' top ten management positions. Armed personnel were being assigned to each manager and those security units would stay with the manager they are assigned to 24/7 until the issue of those deaths has been cleared.

The Security Director had also covered the loss of control at the base where Albert Aberdeen was being held. At that time, they had not been able to regain access to the base. The fact a situation was ongoing there had not gotten out and they were doing everything possible to make sure that no one outside the company and its security system learned of the standoff.

"Delbert, is it possible, Albert is responsible for those three deaths?"

Delbert stood there looking down at the desk top and then back up to Theodor. "Yes sir, I'm sure of it. I don't know how and I don't know when it started but the fact, he has taken over the base and we are not able to get it back under our control tells me Albert is our number one suspect."

"But how the hell is he doing it Del? If he's tied down in the base, how is he killing those people?"

"Sir, I don't know how he's doing it but I'm sure he is. Frankly it scares the hell out of me. If he is killing those people and is still holed up in the base then he could take out anyone he wants and we wouldn't be able to stop him."

"Good for you Del. I knew you would figure this out in time."

Theodor looked at Del with this look of fear chiseled across his face. Delbert was looking around the room and reaching for his gun at the same time.

"Del, that gun won't help you at all so just pull it out and lay it on the floor. Do it Del and do it now."

There was no one there but they both heard him and they both knew who he was.

"Albert, you're not in charge here. This is my office and you have not been asked to be here, return to your room at the base and do it now."

"Theodor, you need to reconsider what you have just said. Del you're out of your realm here and you know it. Now, the two of you will sit down and hear me out."

Both men were looking around the room while moving back to their chairs and sitting down. They sat there waiting for Albert to continue. At that moment a figure started to appear at the side of the desk away from the windows.

They watched as the figure became more and more distinct and clear. They recognized him and still were shocked by the shape and size of his head. He stood there looking at them. "Quite the sight, don't you think? When you put me in that room you figured you had total control over me and you left me there. The only thing I had there in that room was my mind and I spent all my time there in my mind growing and learning.

"During that time, I went through a mutation and this is what resulted. My mind, gentlemen, had taken on the challenge of being isolated like that and it grew and reached out and now I am what I am. Whether you knew it or not you made me what you see here now. You gave me the control and ability to take my revenge against all of you and that thing you call a Super Train.

"Oh, you need to know the train is a failure. It will never work and the power plant will destroy itself when you try the test run. All the money and years put into that train will be lost.

"But I need to tell you, you will not be there to see it. Right now, you are about to face your judgment and I'm the judge."

They sat there looking at him with a bewildered look in their faces. Theodor then leaned forward. "Albert, do you know you're insane?"

Albert smiled at him and took a step back and looked up at the ceiling and then back at the two of them. "Of course, I'm insane. Only an insane man would be pursuing the level of revenge I'm after. Of course, I'm insane after being held in that room for the last thirty years with no one to talk to or have a relationship with.

"Of course, I'm insane after being dragged away from my life and having everything I valued and love stripped from me. What the hell did you expect anyway?"

"Albert, we didn't realize what was happening to you. If we had known we would have taken the proper steps to help you and insure your mental wellbeing."

"Shut up Theodor. I've heard all the crap in the world from the likes of you and I don't think I need to hear any more.

"All you need to know is now, right this moment; you are going to receive what you've earned. You're going to die and I've picked a unique way in which the two of you are going to die."

Without any warning the two of them stood up and moved around to the end of the desk next to the windows. Del reached out

229

and grabbed Theodor by the neck and started to throttle him.

At the same time Theodor reached out and grabbed Del by the neck and started choking him. The two of them stood there slowly increasing the amount of pressure on each other's throat, they were staring each other in the face and applying the pressure to the other, slowly increasing their grips.

Being the younger and more powerful man, Del's pressure was adjusted to match that of Theodor's so they both were experiencing the same results at the same time.

It was maybe three minutes later when the two of them dropped to their knees. Both were trying to scream but they could not get the breath needed to be able to scream.

The pressure increased as they fell over on their sides and continued until both bodies became silent. There was no more movement or sign of breathing from either one. Albert remained there for several minutes watching the bodies and making sure they were in fact dead."…

The next day the headlines presented the dual death of two of the Super Train executives. I sat there looking at the article and thought to myself how terrible their deaths must have been. Albert was truly taking his revenge.

Just then I felt Albert's presence, "How we doing David?"

It was so nonchalant it shocked me. "Albert, do you know and understand what you have done to those people?"

I sat there waiting for an answer and then it came. "Of course, I do David. I'm killing them one at a time and I'm doing it in ways no one has ever seen or heard of before. Besides, they're getting what they deserve."

"Albert, is there anything I can say that will stop this madness?"

"David, David, I can see you still don't understand what is going on here do you? After all I've shown you and all you have learned you still don't see what is going on here?

"David, my patience is wearing thin with you. We've gone over this and you have agreed to stay put and let me finish this process. You came here to stop a disaster from happening if I set off the vortex and I have agreed with your logic on that issue, but you still think these men need to be left as they are.

"Damn, you make me so mad I could just set everything off. You're trying my patience and I'm just fractions away from letting it all go."

"Albert please, I'm having a hard time with this whole mess. Albert, I'm sorry if, I caused you concerns and problems, but you're killing people just as if it were a game to you. I find that hard to deal with."

I felt my mind relax and knew he had stepped away from me. All I could do was sit there and wait for him to return and find out just how bad I had made things.

Damn, I needed to learn this thing was on a track and it was going to finish no matter what I thought or said. Every time I opened my mouth, I made things that much worse. "Albert, I need to talk to you."

"What is it?"

"Albert, I understand what you've gone through and I know I'm a pain in the ass. I also know I can't change things; this thing is on a roll and it has to go to its ending. I will say nothing more concerning your reasons or actions and will remain here and wait for you to return for me."

"Thank you, David. Please relax; you and your family are not in danger. Trust me. I'll make sure nothing bad befalls any of you."

With that the paper read out started to move again and it came to a head line that read. "Chief Attorney for Grand Futures INC. the designer and builder of the Super Train was found dead this evening in his car in the parking lot of the Grand Futures INC. main plant."

…"Good evening Mr. Morgan, have a good weekend."

"Thank you, Mary, and the same for you."

Morgan moved down the hall heading for the elevator when he heard someone calling his name. "Mr. Morgan, can I see you for a minute?"

He turned and there was his law clerk running down the hall toward him. "Sure Max, what can I do for you?"

Sir, well that research you wanted done on the Albert Aberdeen issue, I think we may have a problem with the whole mess. Do you have a few minutes to go over it with me?"

"Yeah, let's step into the library and take care of it.

"Now, what's the problem?"

"Well, as you know you wanted me to make sure all the legal paper work on the control and maintenance of Albert was correct and in their proper order."

"That's right, what's the problem?"

"Sir, I don't know how to say this but someone has been screwing with our document files on the Aberdeen issue."

"How's that?"

"Several of the documents have been altered and actually say the opposite of what they originally said. I have gone over those documents before and I know what they said and it's all been turned around. If anyone saw those papers today, we'd be in deep shit."

"First of all, no one is going to see anything. Got that?"

"Yes sir."

"Second, I want the entire file placed in my office safe so it will be controlled over the weekend. When I get back Monday we will deal with the issue and find out who the hell is playing around."

"Yes sir, I'll see to that before I leave."

"Thank you, Max, and have a good weekend."

"Yes sir, I will."

Morgan left the library and when he got to the first floor, he exited onto the parking lot and walked out to his car.

It was a pleasant evening. The sky was clear and there was a light breeze drifting across the lot.

When he got to his car, he opened it and got in. The moment he entered the car a figure appeared in the passenger seat next to him. The sudden appearance of this person shocked the hell out of him. A second shock came when he recognized the person and saw the shape of his head.

"Albert, what the hell are you doing here and what the hell happened to your head?"

Albert sat there looking out the windshield of the car. He didn't say a word; he just sat there for several seconds. He slowly turned his head toward Morgan. "Paul, how the hell are you?"

The question was not what Morgan expected and he answered. "I'm fine Albert, now what are you doing here?"

"Paul, you know what I'm doing here, now don't you?"

There was silence as Morgan sat there thinking about what had been going on with Albert over the years and somehow, he had managed to get off the base and ended up in his car. "Albert, I have no idea as to what is going on. Maybe you better fill me in?"

A smile moved across Albert's face as he reached over and placed his hand on the back of Morgan's right hand. It was like a fire brand had been placed on Morgan's right hand and he withered in pain. "Albert, what the hell are you doing? That hurts like hell."

Albert slowly removed his hand and then looked directly at Morgan. "That's to let you know what is taking place here is more than just a talk. You have been working closely with the Grand Future Company in dealing with my incarceration. You know what the hell they have been doing to me and that means you approved every move they made."

Morgan sat there thinking he needed to get the hell out of that car and away from Albert as soon as he could. Just as he thought that the car door next to him locked. "Paul, you and I have an appointment with destiny,

236

right here and right now. It's time for you to pay for your misdeeds. It's time for you to face justice, my justice."

The death of all the others flashed across Morgan's mind as Albert was saying that. "Albcrt, you can't be serious. My job with Grand Futures is strictly as an advisor. I have no control over what they do or how they do it. All I can do as their advisor is warn them if they are going down the wrong path and, in your case, they did just that. Albert, I warned them and they didn't heed my warning."

It fell quiet as Albert sat there looking out the window. How was he going to deal with this man, this lying sack of shit? He knew full well what was going on and advised them as to how they could cover their actions. He turned toward Morgan. "You seem to be an intelligent man. I can tell in the way you handle yourself and your speech mannerism.

"However, there is one problem you failed to cover and that is the fact everything you have said so far is a sack of shit.

"You knew what they were doing to me and you guided them in the legal issues they had to cover while dealing with me. You sat back and took your retainer fees and let them tear my life out of me and leave me to become the creature I am today. For that you are going to pay."

Morgan started to say something when his car started all by itself. He reached down and tried to turn the key off but it would not move. He then tried to open the car door and it would not open.

He looked over at Albert. "Look, you're all messed up and you're doing the wrong thing. I'm not your enemy, the company is. I'm just a paid employee and that's all I am. Now stop this nonsense now and leave me alone."

Albert sat there looking out the window and then he looked at the man he was killing. "No, you're a direct part in this and for that I'm going to cook you alive."

He then reached over and turned the heat in the car to full heat and then disappeared. Morgan sat there shaking his head and reached over to turn the heat off but the controls would not move.

Already the temperature in the car was increasing and he was feeling the effect. He knew it could never get hot enough to actually roast him, but he still didn't want to stay in the car.

He again tried to open the door and then turned toward the passenger door and brought his feet up and started to kick the window. He couldn't break the glass. As hard as he kicked the glass held firm.

It was starting to get a lot hotter in the car than he had imagined it could ever get. In fact, when he touched the steering wheel, he burned his hand. Damn, this was nuts. No car could get hot enough to roast a person that was impossible.

He felt himself starting to panic and looking around for people walking by his car. He tried to honk the horn and again burned his hand and the horn failed to honk. Finally, he saw Max walking by his car and he started to kick the back window. Max looked over, seeing his boss he ran to the driver's door and looked in.

The motor was running and he could hear the heater running as well. When he took hold of the door handle it burned his hand. He backed off and seeing a security unit driving by he hailed them. They stopped and approached the car and seeing the situation they took their batons and tried to break the window out.

In the car Morgan was finding it harder and harder to breath. He had stopped sweating and his skin was starting to redden up. He was taking his clothes off to try and reduce the amount of heat but it didn't help. He had finally removed the last of his clothes and found the seat was getting so hot that too was burning him. He was slowly becoming more lethargic and finally passed out."…

I finished reading the article and thinking about what that man had gone through in that car. Albert had cooked him to death. It had to have been one of the worst ways to die anyone had ever heard of.

I then let the paper scanning start moving again and it progressed one week and then stopped. The next head line told me everything. "CEO of Grand Futures INC. Found Dead" I started to read the article.

…"What I want to know is when the hell are you going to get into that base and kill that little pig anyway? He's killed half a dozen people and if this goes much longer, he'll be coming after me."

"Mr. Tylor, we're doing everything we can but he has the base locked down. Every unit we have sent in had stopped communicating. When we fly over, we can see their bodies. If we try to land the aircraft it's blown up. He has the place tied down tight. I don't think we could get in no matter what wc did."

"Then you need to increase the security around the management teams of the company. So far, you've failed in that issue as well.

"I'm not going to become one of his wins, do you understand me. I'll blow that entire base up if I have to but he will not get to me. So, you had better get your act together and start doing what I pay you for. Do you understand?"

"Yes sir, we have been trying in every way possible to ensure your safety. We have every entrance to this place covered with multiple teams. We have roving teams moving through the grounds and on every floor with the order to shoot to kill anyone who should not be at any location they don't belong.

"Sir, we have every base covered. I just don't know what else we can do."

The headquarters of the Grand Futures main administration building was like a fortress. At every door coming into the building there were shock teams. Not just one but two and three. No one was going to gain entry unless they wanted them to.

A shadow passed across the desk in front of Tylor and his Chief of Security. They both looked at it as it moved across the desk and then across the floor and up the wall. It was a full figure of a man standing there.

The Chief stepped around the desk and positioned himself between the shadow and Mr. Tylor. Nothing happened for several minutes. The Chief keyed his radio mic and called for a shock team to report to the CEO's office.

There was no reply. He tried again and then realized his radio was dead. "Yeah, I killed it when I came in the office.

They both looked at the shadow and then started to back across the room toward the door. As they approached the door, they heard the latch being thrown. The Chief reached back and tried to turn the lock bar and it would not move.

The Shadow remained stationary but appeared to be turning and watching them trying to get out of the office. "You know you can't avoid me don't you Tylor. None of the others could either. You have no idea what you have created and what it means to you and this company.

"Because of your greed you tried to sock me away for future use and then you forgot about me. You let mc languish in that base for years, not caring one bit about me and my welfare. All I had was me and my mind and we changed in that time. We changed like nothing you could ever imagine.

"You knew you had me and anytime you wanted to you could bring me out of cold storage and use me. But you forgot about my mind. You failed to realize my mind was far more dangerous than my physical being.

"You didn't see the mind as it started to deal with the isolation and the loneliness you forced it into. It grew and dwelled on its situation and then it started to grow. It started to create. It started to imagine. It slowly went mad and then in that madness it mutated. It was through that mutation my mind became a force you would never be able to deal with. A force so powerful it has completely destroyed the Super Train and now it is destroying those who did this to me.

"I want you to understand what you have done. I want you to know all the money

243

you have gained will mean nothing to you in the long run. I want you to suffer like none other has ever suffered. I want you to know the depth of my hate for you, for those who worked for you and helped you and for that damn train and all it stands for."

They were trapped and they knew it. This man, this being standing there in the form of a shadow was crazy to the extreme. A feeling of hopelessness washed through them as they realized the helplessness of their situation.

"Albert, I can only keep track of so much. I have to depend on people below me to keep me informed as to what is going on. Albert, they failed to do that. I'm as much a victim as you are. I didn't know what they were doing to you and what was resulting.

"I'm just one man and it's impossible for me to know everything and keep track of everything. I'm at the mercy of those below me and if they fail in their duties to me and to you, then you and I are left in the lurch. Albert, I had no idea as to what they were doing to you and what was happening to you."

"You're a liar. Don't stand there and think you can con me. I have been here in this office for the last two hours watching and listening to you. I heard everything you said to your Chief Security Officer and I heard everything he said to you.

"If there's a victim other than me in this room it is that Security Officer you're standing behind. Yet he still knew what he was doing in carrying out your orders.

"No, the two of you are guilty as charged and you will both face your punishment here and now."

Just then the shadow moved away from the wall and formed into a man. He was recognized immediately as being Albert Aberdeen except his head was grotesque. It was misshapen by the growth of his brain and the expansion of his mental abilities.

The Chief went for his gun and as it came out it continued up to his head and stopped with the barrel against his head and his hand on the trigger. He tried to pull it down but could not move it.

Albert walked over to him looking him straight in the eyes. "Damn, you people will never learn. Your old-fashioned methods are useless against me. That gun might as well be used on you.

"How does it feel? Is the barrel cold or warm? Is it hard against your head? How much trigger pull will it take to fire that gun and send a slug through your brain?"

The Chief was sweating and starting to cry. "Please, don't do this. I don't know how we can repay you for all that has happened to you, but you've got to give us a chance at repayment."

"Damn you people are all the same. When you're faced with your punishment you all, to the man, have agreed with my assessment of my mistreatment. You agree with everything I have said and you're willing to make corrections.

"Don't you understand there is no correction for what you have done to me? There is no money value you can come up with that will pay for what has happened to me. Can't you see all your useless offers absolutely can't change anything for me?

"I am what I am and it is permanent. I am insane and that is permanent. I look as I look and that is permanent. There is nothing you can say or nothing you can do will change any of this. As a result, that leaves me with only one course of action and that is retribution. That's what I'm here for."

The Chief was standing there with his gun at his head when his trigger finger started to squeeze the trigger. "No, Albert please I beg you don't do this. I've done nothing to you, why are you doing this to me?"

The trigger finger relaxed and Albert walked toward them. "You didn't do anything to me? You didn't order those teams to try and take me out? You didn't run that camp for the full purpose of keeping me isolated and trapped? You didn't once come to see me and check to see if I needed anything or to check my welfare?

"Sorry but you're just as guilty as the thing standing behind you. It's time."

The trigger finger tightened and the gun recoiled and fell out of the Chiefs hand. They both hit the floor at the same moment.

Morgan stood there holding his hands up in front of face with his head turned to the left and his face looking down at the body on the floor in front of him. "Albert, please, there has to be some way for me to help you and bring all this killing to an end. I can give you anything you want from anywhere in the world. All you need to do is ask. Please, give me a chance."

247

Albert looked up from the body and directly into Morgan's eyes. "Why is it you people suddenly feel you have failed me and are willing to give me anything I want when just minutes ago you were berating that man for not killing me?

"You're all a bunch of hypocrites and each of you deserves to die. You have held me for thirty years and I only wish I could make your punishment last thirty years. No, you're going to die now and the world will be a better place as a result.

"You just don't see what you have done. I was a nothing to you. I was a commodity; a brain trust you needed to control and keep from the rest of the world. It was my brain you wanted to control and the rest of me was just so much garbage. Well now look what you've made.

"I'm insane as hell and will never change. My mind is running wild and I will never come to a point of complete and total control. So, I've decided to let it run. I've decided to let my mind have it's time of glory and you and all the others have done this to me will pay with your lives.

"Damn this feels good. Morgan, how the hell do you want to die?"

Morgan was backed up against the door by now. His face was a reflection of the fear that was coursing through his mind. "Albert, I don't want to die. God man what can I do to get you to drop this vendetta of yours? Please, give me a chance."

That set Albert off. "Chance, what the hell kind of a chance did you give me? You don't know the rage that was building in me. I've got to release it and this is the only way I know how. Damn you for making me this way."

Just then Albert's face went dark and his eye narrowed. The rage swirling around, Albert was out of control. Slowly Morgan began to slide down the face of the door as his body was being eviscerated from one end to the other.

Thirty years of torture was being released on that body. Thirty years of fear and loneliness. When Albert left there were two bodies on the floor, one the Chief with one bullet hole through his head and the other one Morgan Tylor."…

CHAPTER TWELVE

The Deal

The paper headlines moved on to the current date and the end of the article on the killings of personnel of the Grand Futures, INC. I sat back letting my mind recover from the on slot of information and the grisly accounts of all those who had died.

I must have sat there for ten minutes or so when he came to me. "David, I see you have read all the accounts of my accomplishments. What do you think of them?"

I wasn't prepared to talk to Albert at this time, but I knew better than to brush him off. "Albert, I don't know. I'm still trying to let it all sink in. I don't know if I want to talk about them any time soon."

"Yes, I can understand that. I must admit I lost my temper in a couple of those events. But for the most part they all paid a price for their treachery.

"The problem with this whole mess David is I don't feel any sense of satisfaction. I don't know if I did them in too fast or I didn't do enough to them, know what I mean?"

"No Albert, I don't know what you mean. I don't know if you were justified in what you did to those people. I know you took your revenge but I don't know if your revenge was the right thing to do."

"Interesting David, I hadn't expected you to react this way. You seem a little too calm and controlled. I expected more anger and rage from you. What's going on David? What are you really thinking?"

Those were two good questions and I was afraid I didn't have a good answer for them, at least not right now. I got up and walked to the front door and on out onto the front lawn. I walked over to a bench next to one of Lisa's flower beds and sat down. He was there. He had accompanied me out of the house.

"Albert, I want to answer you truthfully, but I fear you will not take it right and as a result you may take added actions against those you hate so much or against me and my family."

"David, I have told you I would not harm you or your family and I mean that. I know you're having a difficult time with what I have done and I think that it is important you are having such a difficult time.

"I am now ready to sit down with you and layout my remaining plans. I want you to go to your children and other person, that Paul person, and arrange to come together so I can lay out everything to you and bring this whole thing to an end. Will you do that this evening at seven?"

This was it; he was now ready to finalize this mess I found myself in. "Yes Albert, I can do that. We will meet at my youngest daughter's house at that time. What then?"

"At that time David, I will bring you here to me and we will work the remainder of my plan out. Relax David; it's not going to be as bad as you think."

With that I walked back in to my daughter's house and waited for her to arrive home after getting off work. When she arrived home, I told her of the need for the next meeting.

She called the others and set up the meeting. We fixed our dinner and prepared to leave for Jean's place.

At seven we were all there and I advised them what was to take place at that time. "I will be going to Albert's location again. He has told me this will be the last meeting and it will cover the completion of his plan. He advised when I come back from that meeting everything will be coming to an end and he will be cleaning things up."

Paul sat there looking at me. "Do you believe him David?"

I thought the question over for a few seconds and then looked at Paul. "Yeah Paul, I do. I think he has something unusual in store for me. I don't believe he is planning on harming me, he has told me several times he would not do that. No, he has something odd and special in mind and I think I need to hear him out."

The others were watching Paul and me as we discussed the coming meeting with

Albert. Finally, Pat spoke up. "Dad, has he given you even a hint as to what he is going to address at this meeting tonight?"

"Pat, other than saying this was going to be the last meeting. No, he has given me nothing that would give us any idea as to what he is up to. Even if he had, I still must go to this meeting. I don't think we can avoid it and if we tried then I think we would only exacerbate the problem. No, I have to go."

I looked at the clock and it was five minutes to seven. I looked at Paul and nodded my head. He pulled out the syringe and prepped it with the drug he had used earlier.

I positioned myself on the couch and he administered the drug and I settled back. I thought to myself, "Albert I'm ready."

Almost as soon as the thought hit my mind, I found myself in Albert's room sitting on the chair I had been in before.

"Thank you, David, for being so punctual. We have a lot to do and little time to do it in.

"David, you have been wondering why I brought you here this far into your future and now I can tell you. David, I wanted you to personally witness what happened to me and

254

what actions I have taken against those who have done this to me.

"It is important you see that and understand what has taken place. It is going to be the key to everything you do from here on out. Over the next few hours, I am going to give you a considerable amount of information concerning everything you have seen and the people that have been involved. It is important you commit this information to your mind and you retain it.

"David, I must emphasize to you just how important the next few hours are going to be. If you fail to take this seriously then what will come thirty years after I was abducted will in fact happen. David, it will be the end of this world.

"I am going to give you a chance to rewrite this time you are visiting. How things happen in this time frame will be totally up to how well you do your job in your time.

"Everything you have gone through to this point has been the precursor to what you are going to learn right now.

"David, I want you to know I love you and I consider you as my brother, but thirty years ago you had the opportunity to stop my abduction and you failed to do so.

"They threatened you and your family, and you folded in front of them and that condemned me to the last thirty years of hell. From my perspective David, you were the one element in this whole nasty mess that is responsible for me being as I am. For that I am going to make you face your responsibilities to me and this world of ours.

"At first I was angry at you and wanted to kill you just as I did those others. But my love for you refused to let me do that, so I decided to force you into action for both yours and my futures.

"David, I am not going to harm you. In some respects what I am going to do will be much more severe. You failed me at that moment when I needed you the most. It has taken me all this time to deal with my attitude toward you and bring myself to this action."

He sat there looking at me and waiting for me to respond. Hell, I was having one heck of a time just trying to grasp the situation I was facing. He was holding me responsible for all that has happened to him and all those others over the last thirty years. That includes my kids and wife Helen. How the hell could he do that?

"Albert, I don't understand. How can you hold me responsible for something others did to you? Albert, it doesn't make any sense at all. They, the corporation, were the ones who took you and did this thing to you. How can that translate into holding me accountable for their actions?"

He smiled at me then stood up and started pacing back and forth in front of me. "David, you have conveniently chosen to forget about what really happened on that day I was taken. Your guilt has drawn a shadow in front of you and you have hidden from the truth and reality of what took place.

"Let me tell you what happened and then you will remember."

"It was June 2014 and we had just finished putting together the final figures on the power plant for the Super Train. It had been almost three years in the process and we had worked our hearts out to achieve that one goal.

"The original concept of the power plant had been yours, and once you had laid it out for me, I understood what you were working toward. I realized you needed me to put the actual mathematics together for the project and once that was done, we would be

257

able to supply a system that could take the train to speeds that were unthinkable.

"It was four thirty that afternoon when you picked the phone up and quietly dialed a number. When the party answered all, you said was "It's complete." Then you hung up. I thought nothing of it and finished getting my things together so I could head home and enjoy the weekend.

"I asked if you wanted to go for a beer and you said you had a number of things you needed to do, tying up some loose ends and for me to go ahead and you would follow.

"I thought it strange at the time but shrugged it off and headed for the bar. I never made it. They met me at the elevator on the first floor as I exited it and started for the front doors.

"It was a team of four men who walked up to me and kept me moving over to the stairs and then into the stairwell and down into the executive parking garage. There they hit me with a load of drugs and the last thing I recall was being placed into the back seat of a car. The next thing I remember is waking up lying on a bed in a small room.

"I know now you knew what was going to happen and you were to stay out of the way while they took me. David, I think the stress and shock of what happened drove you into a state of selective amnesia. I really think you did not know or understand what had happened. That your mind would not accept the fact you had been a part of my abduction and you preferred to drive that memory into a closed place in your mind and lock it in there.

"David, you of all people hurt me the most. We had worked together and played together and you turned on me when the chips were down. I swore that the day would come when I would kill you for what you had done. But as time passed and my mind mutated, I began to understand what had happened. I knew then I would use you at the right time to change all this and give me my freedom.

"David, all you have heard about, read about, and talked about over the last thirty years from the moment I took you and you disappeared to this point in time can be changed. In order to do that you will have to be the one who changes it.

"David, you are going to be sent back to that point when my abduction took place and you are going to take the action then you should have taken. I am going to send you back one week prior to the abduction and in

259

that one week you will work to reverse all that has happened in the past thirty years.

"If you're successful, then all that has happened in these past thirty years will change. You will not disappear. I will not have been abducted. Your children will not have to live those thirty years without you, and you will have the means of saving Helens life from cancer.

"If you fail, then all that has happened will happen just as you have learned. However, the creation of the vortex will take place as well and this world will come to an end.

"There you have it David. You will have one week to stop my abduction and if you fail then the thirty years that is behind us here will happen and you will be the sole person responsible. That David is my retribution for what you did to me.

"Now I am going to place in your mind information about the Executive Officers of the Grand Futures, INC. What I give you will be so private they can never deny what you are telling them.

"David, you must convince the heads of the company to drop their plans for me and in doing that you will save all that is dear and meaningful to you."

I felt him enter my mind and then the images and secrets of the executive officers of the company entered my mind. Everything was there, every piece of information and details I would need to demonstrate to those people I knew what I was talking about.

When he finished, all I could do was sit there looking at him. He was right and I could remember just what he was talking about. It all came back to me and I felt the pain of my corruption wash over me. I had been responsible for the success of his abduction and now he was taking his revenge on me. If all came to an end it would be at my hands and not his. I would die knowing I had set the ground work for this final act.

He then sat back. "David, I know the pressure you were under and I understand why you took the easy way out. The problem I have with this whole thing is you never ever tried to pursue the issue after that.

"I have thought for many years just how I was going to deal with you and I came to understand to kill you would do little or no good other than harm others. So, I decided to teach you a lesson and put you in a position if you didn't work it out when I sent you back it would have ramifications you could never live with.

"David, you are a good man and even in my insanity I can see that. I still love you as a brother and I know if I have any hope of avoiding this life at this time, I need you to get me out of this. Do you understand?"

He had me and damn-it anyway I had screwed up and he has paid for it all these years. It was becoming clear to me, now he had used Time Trap to bring me into one of the alternative paths that time could take from that moment when Albert was abducted.

Sitting here in this room thirty years later is only one path it could go. If things had happened or could happen at the time of his abduction then this time path would never have taken place.

It was now clear he had planned this whole thing from the moment I fell into Time Trap to this place, at this time. He had provided me with everything that was coming and in doing that he gave me the incentive to take action and pursue the wrong that had been done him.

I sat back and let out a long breath. "You're right Albert; you're right in every aspect of what has happened over these past thirty years. I'm ashamed for what I actually did. It's hard to be forced to remember something you don't want to remember and you selected a rather unique way in bringing me face to face with my actions.

"I don't like it, but I understand and realize now just what my simple inactions have resulted in. I don't know what needs to be done next but I'm ready to take on whatever it is you have planned for me."

"David, I want you to know I am not planning your death. You are the one person who can get me out of this and that is the tradeoff. If I killed you then I would stay as I am and this world would end.

"If I got you to help me then everyone, including those I have killed here in this time will live. All you and I have to do is alter a few actions by ourselves and those who took me and we can change all this for the better. Now does that sound like the action of an insane man?"

That comment almost floored me. The little weasel had conned me. He wasn't insane, he was in control. In his current mental makeup, he could manipulate time and he was playing it for all he was worth.

He had drawn me into this hell and in doing that he opened my mind and forced me to face my past and what really had happened. He was sitting there watching me move through the logical progression of what he had done and the more I moved along the bigger his smile.

"David, I think you're coming to grips with the situation. You're right, I set this whole thing up as a means of getting you to act when you should have.

"Believe me when I tell you this was all a great gamble on my part. You could have responded in any number of ways but you took the right path and now we're on our way to clearing up this whole mess."

I wanted to hit him. I wanted to tear his face off and I wanted him to know it. By the look on his face my feeling had gotten through. "All right Albert, you've had your fun and you've forced me to see what I did wrong, but that still does not change what we are dealing with today. Now where do we go from here?"

"David, I have already told you where this is going. All that needs to be done is for you to return to your awaken state and fill the others in and then I will be sending you back.

"There is one little issue you need to understand. When I send you back it will be to that time when the abduction took place. That point in time when you could and should have stepped in and stopped this whole mess.

"Once that has been done successfully, you will return to the street intersection you drove through and you will slip back into your life and that of your family. Do you understand?"

Oh boy, this was getting more complex every minute. "Albert, can you actually do all that and not foul something up in the process?"

He stood up and walked across the room to a cabinet and opened it and pulled out a notebook. He then returned to his seat and opened the notebook and handed it over to me.

As I sat there reading over the entries, I began to realize this was a second-by-second history of my life from the moment of the abduction to this time he had brought me to. The notebook was only about half an inch thick but as I turned the pages, they progressed from page to page moving through time.

I was holding a portable time line in my hand. The number of years it covered was incalculable. It crossed my mind this simple notebook could go on into the future for as long as I wanted to turn the pages.

"Albert, this is impossible. How can this be a book that covers time?"

"Relax David; it's only a gimmick I have developed so you could see the detail of my abilities to work time. What you need to know is if we are successful in changing the things that happened back to the point when I was abducted, this Albert will never be. Do you understand?

"In a way David, I'm committing suicide here. If I am never abducted, I will never be in the environment that produced this Albert and this mind will never have mutated as you see it now. That David is the size and weight of the task you are faced with."

Insane, no, this was not just insane, this was off the chart insane and to make things even more unbelievable, it is probably the perfect solution to the situation I was facing.

My head was spinning by this time and I really had no idea what was to come next or should come next. I felt him there watching me and he could see my confusion and fear. "Take your time David. You'll do just fine. I've dropped a lot of stuff on you and I know what it is doing to you. You must understand I needed to do it this way in order to make the impression I am driving for.

"All this, David, has been carried out in order to bring you to this point. In order to drive home what you have done, or better yet failed to do. All this has been done in order for you and me to save or to salvage the lives that have been impacted by that abduction. To bring each and every one of them back to a normal and fruitful life, yes even those who had carried out the abduction."

It was then I felt the coming together of the two of us. I don't know if this kind of an elaborate ruse was necessary, but it worked and was actually classic Albert.

We sat there looking at one another and nodding our heads. He finally stood and reached out to me. I took his hand and stood facing him. "All right David, it's time for you to go back to your kids and that Paul person and lay things out to them. Be easy on them because they will find it difficult to understand what is going on.

267

The most important thing is you make it clear to them when you leave this current life will no longer be. The lives they are living right now are actually your life as a result of the time jump. If you are successful you will achieve the goal, I have set for you and the next thirty years from that time you disappeared would change for all and to the better. Are you ready?"

I nodded and squeezed his hand. At that moment I woke up and the four of them were standing there looking down on me. "What, what are all you standing there like that for?"

"Dad, we have been standing here listening to the conversation going on between you and Albert. Dad, it's all been made clear to us and we understand.

"Dad, we know any number of things could happen in any moment or day that would change the future as we approach it. Somehow Albert has been able to project you into your future and the events that have happened here as a result of your personal actions.

"None of us here are angry with you. It was not our life that you were living but we now know why time took the path it did to this point in time some thirty years later."

268

I was dumb founded. Albert had opened everything up and they knew it all. I felt the sting of the situation wash over me and as I sat up all I could do was cry. The three of them sat down beside me and we all had a good long cry.

Finally, I got up and turned toward them. "You now know what has been going on and what I need to do to change this life you have lived. You know when I leave here and go back to that time you and this time frame will no longer exist.

"That does not mean you won't end up in this exact life at some point in my future, but the odds are good you will not. I will strive to ensure that I remain with you and mom and we will have a good life as a family. If I fail in this task, I will tell you this, you will know what happened to me.

"If I die while trying to carry out this task you will live a life without me, but you will know what happened to me and why it happened and that is far better than never knowing."

I turned to Paul and reached out and took his hand. "I want to thank you for your help. I know you're trying to deal with the fact when I leave here you will not be. It is my honest hope sometime in my life as I move through time you and I meet again and form a good friendship. I think when we meet, we will recognize the connection we have between us now."

I then turned back to the kids. "All right now, it's time for me to get to work. I have two reasons for going back and taking on this whole mess. One is so that you, my children, can live a life that at least will tell you what happened to your dad. The other is so Albert can live the life he deserves to live and not the terror this life has burdened him with."

I then walked up to Pat and put my arms around him and kissed him on the cheek. We stood there holding one another for several seconds and then I backed away and turned toward Jane.

The tears were running down her cheeks as I reached out and pulled her close to me. I could feel she had been the one hurt the most by my disappearance those many years ago. I held her close and then kissed her on the cheek and told her I loved her.

Finally, I turned to Lisa. She had this small smile on her face. She had always known I had never run from her and the others and that belief had been confirmed. As

I held her, I thought of Helen and knew I would be successful in this task I was about to set out to complete.

I held Lisa at arm's length. "You kids will know nothing of this moment but I will. I will know what you will grow up to be and how close you are to one another. I want you to know I will be an active part of your lives, every minute and every second. For that I would move heaven and earth."

I then stepped back and looked around. "All right Albert, I'm ready."

I didn't know what to expect when he started the time reversal. It could have been just about anything from a great explosion to a flash of light to an earthquake. The fact was I found myself sitting at my desk looking across the desk at Albert. It was just that simple and I actually could remember all that had happened in the other time frame, in Time Trap.

I looked at the calendar on my desk and it was one year prior to the June day of my disappearance. From that moment on I would be rebuilding my future.

CHAPTER THIRTEEN

A New Life for All

"David, I think we are almost finished with the power plant. It's been one hell of a job but I feel good about it, how about you?"

"I don't know Albert. I still have a couple of reservations about some of our calculations, but for all intent and purposes I agree it's about as done as we're going to see it."

He, Albert, was looking the office area over and tapping his fingers of both hands on the arms of the chair he was sitting in. "We've been working in this office for five years and I'm just about ready to find someplace else to hang out. The fact is I'll be back here tomorrow to start our next project.

"By the way, the others were heading over to Jack's Bar for some pizza and beer, you planning on coming?"

I sat there looking at him and wondering if he knew what was going to happen here in just a few minutes, or did he leave this situation entirely to me to carry out the changes needed to be made. "Yeah, I think I'll call Helen and run by and get her. I think she would like the chance to be in on our success.

"She spent a lot of time home alone while you and I worked on this thing and I think she deserves the recognition as well."

Albert was nodding his head and then stood and started for the door. "I have to run up to the admin offices. They have a couple of questions about the layout of our presentation they wanted answered. Should only take a few minutes and then I'll be over to the bar."

I got up and moved around the desk and over by the door and placed my hand on the door knob and looked right at Albert. "No, you're not going up to the admin offices. You and I are going to leave this place right now and you're not going to ask any questions until we're free of this building, got me?"

He was shocked at the quickness of my actions and my forceful attitude toward him. "What is it David? What's going on?"

"Albert, I have known for some time now they are planning on reassigning you to another facility. The fact is Albert, they are going to kidnap you and place you into a restricted base.

"They have been planning this all along. I only just recently discovered it and when you said you had been called to the admin office; I knew they were going to make their moves now. Albert, I'm not playing a game here, they are actually planning on kidnapping you. Do you understand me?

Their plan is to give you an envelope they want you to take with you when you leave. You are to place the envelope on the main entry desk for the security officer at that location. He will open the envelope and is to give you a package. At that time four men will move in on you and you will be taken down in the basement and transported to their base and held there from then on.

He relaxed his grip on the door knob and started to nod his head. "Yeah, I had a feeling their reason for me to go up there was rather lame. You're sure of this?"

274

"Yeah, I'm sure of it. I wasn't too sure when I first heard about it, but this meeting tells me they are actually going to do it. So, let's get the hell out of here and we'll figure out our actions once we're clear of this place."

"David, what about the main gate, surely they will have the guards notified about me and not to let me off the plant site?"

"I know and we won't be going through any of the manned gates. Now grab a bundle of those papers over there and come with me."

We walked out the door and turned toward the main planning center. Between my office and that location there were three doors that would take us out of the building I selected the last one and walked through the lobby area to the back of the lobby and through the door toward the document storage rooms.

We passed through that door and turned left and walked to the end of the hallway and then out onto the parking lot. I had moved my car by that door early that morning. We got in the car and I headed into the plant proper.

I drove through the main plant area and out the other side. I knew of a single gate located at the far end of the runway that was never guarded but was locked. As we approached the gate, I could see there was no one there and then drove up to the gate and placed my bumper against it and stepped on the gas. I was able to break the lock on the third try and we passed on through and headed for town.

I looked over at Albert. "I figure we have maybe twenty minutes before they start to wonder what happened to you. That should give us time to get to a safe house for you."

"What do you mean by a safe house?"

"Albert, we need to find a place where you can hole up until they finally stop looking for you. I figure we have maybe a month before things really get bad. In that time, I will have to meet with the boss and lay the situation out to him and hopefully get them to pull away from their plans."

"You really think you can do that?"

"Yes, Albert I do. I have a few things they will be highly interested in and it should get their attention."

I knew where I was taking him. While I had been in Time Trap, Albert had instilled in my mind the location that would be the safest for him. It would take us about two hours to get there before I could start my next step.

About an hour out I looked over at Albert and he was smiling. "Albert, you know what's going on, here don't you?"

He turned toward me still smiling. "Yes David, I do. I'm just enjoying the situation. Frankly you're doing a fine job and I really think we're going to succeed."

"You had doubts?"

"David, there is always the unknown in every plan and endeavor. This is no different. The unknown is always there and that is what makes the situation challenging."

"All right, you know what is going on but you are not able to interfere or take any actions on your own?"

"No, I cannot do that. I know what is coming and I know what you need to do but I can do nothing to help facilitate the actual actions that needs to be taken. No, you will have to take me to the safe house and leave me. Then it's all up to you.

Now, that is not all of it. I am still the Albert you met in Time Trap and that Albert will be taking part in this process. The Albert you are looking at will not and cannot be involved in this situation. But, the Albert from Time Trap can and will be involved.

"And by the way David, I trust you and I'm sure you will succeed."

We finally reached the safe house and Albert got out and walked toward the house. Halfway there he turned and waved at me and smiled then turned and walked up to the door and into the house.

I returned to the city and headed for Jack's Bar and settled in with the other people there.

It was maybe twenty minutes later when two men walked through the door. They were both dressed in dark suits. Both were well built and clearly could handle themselves. The two of them walked over to my table and one walked around to where I was sitting leaned over to my ear. "Mr. Jacobs, Mr. Tylor wishes to see you. Would you please come along with us?"

I nodded my head and took another bite of pizza and stood and walked toward the door. Pete called out. "Hay David, will you be coming back here?"

I looked back at him and then looked at my watch. "Pete, if I'm not back in two hours then no I won't. If I don't come back, I'll see you in the morning."

"All right boss, see you later."

We left the bar and I got in the front seat of the car and we headed for the administration offices building on the plant site.

Ten minutes later I was walking through the front door wondering if I would ever come back out.

As we entered Mr. Tylor's office there was one other person standing off to the side of the desk. It was Tylor's Chief of Security. He motioned me toward the chair across from him and the other two men left the room.

"Good evening David, how goes it?"

I shifted in my chair and responded. "It's going fine sir. Is there something I can do for you?"

He sat there a minute. "First of all, David, you can drop the innocent thing, it doesn't become you. Where's Albert?"

There it was the key to dealing with Tylor, the direct approach he was so well known for. I sat there looking at him and then over at the Chief and then back to Tylor. I decided to be direct and not delay this anymore than needed. "Mr. Tylor, the first

279

time you abducted Albert I choose to do nothing. That sir was the wrong thing for me to do and I have regretted it ever since."

He looked at me like I had just said something out of line or confusing to him. "What do you mean, 'the first time?"

I had to smile and then continued on. "Tylor, I'm going to tell you a story you will find hard to understand or believe for that matter. But I think you need to know the whole of the situation you and I are faced with.

"Now, we can go ahead and carry on with your Chief here or we can ask him to leave and you and I can deal directly with this issue."

Tylor sat there looking at me. I knew he was working his position and trying to determine whether or not I could or would be a threat to him. Finally, he looked at the Chief and nodded for him to leave.

The Chief nodded back, and then looked at me and turned and walked out the door. Morgan, that was Tylor's first name, then placed both hands on his desk top and leaned toward me. "Now you little ass just what the hell are you up to?"

I had expected some form of attack by him. He had to gain the upper hand and maneuver me into a position of threat. That would give him the better chance of working me into a trap or at the worst, getting up and trying to leave.

"First of all, may I call you Morgan?"

He nodded his head. "If it will get this thing moving then I have no problem with that."

"Thank you and you can call me David if you like." He nodded to me.

"Would you please get started? What is it you have to say?"

"Morgan, I have just returned from a most unpleasant journey. During that journey I met my children and learned my wife Helen was dead. I also met Albert Aberdeen. At the time he was being held prisoner by this company and had been for thirty years."

"What the hell are you talking about? Are you going to sit there thinking you can drop a story like that on me and I would believe it?"

I raised my hands. "Morgan, pull your horns in, what I am telling you I can prove. All I'm asking you to do is sit there and listen. I can assure you when I'm done you will

281

believe me and not only that you will change your plan of action.

"Now let me continue. On June 6 of 2015 I was returning home from going to the post office. When I got to the last intersection just up the street from my house something happened to me, I too found hard to believe.

"I passed through a time warp. I would later learn it was a Time Trap and I was taken thirty years into the future. The next thing I knew I was being arrested and then later released to my three children all of whom were thirty years older.

"Those kids had grown up without their father. The fact was their father had disappeared and was never heard from again until that day thirty years later. I can assure you Morgan the shock of seeing those kids older than me almost killed me. I was confused, scared and knowing nothing as to what had happened to me.

"To cut a long story short I eventually met the individual who had taken me to that time and place through his Time Trap. That individual was Albert Aberdeen. He played a number of mind games with me at first but finally he took me to where he was being held.

"Morgan, he had been housed and held at the companies Sidney base for thirty years from the time of his abduction by you and your administrative team. The part of this meeting that was the most terrifying to me was when I saw Albert. He had mutated and had an elongated head. His brain had grown to a point he could actually control time.

"I was at a loss as to why he had taken me, but I learned in a short time I was taken because I had failed to stand up against you and your team when you abducted that man and placed him in an isolated location and then left him there. You need to know if you actually do find him and abduct him that will result in his going insane.

"Albert then let it be known because of my failure to stand up to you I was also responsible for what he was going to do. Morgan, he was planning on destroying the Super Train when you made the test run from New York to Bradford. The issue there was if he actually did destroy that machine it would cause a vortex that would ultimately destroy the entire world.

"By this time, he had already started to kill off your administrative team. The last one he forced me to witness was when he killed you and your Chief of Security. Morgan, in your case he tore you apart. He ripped your face open and then started in on your body. When he had finished your Chief was dead with a single self-administered gunshot wound to his head and you next to him a pile of mangled meat."

I stopped and sat there looking at Tylor to try and get a measure as to how he was taking my story. He was looking right at me not moving and listening hard. I continued. "Albert then told me he would be sending me back to this point in time to contact you and advise you as to what the future will bring for you if you take the action you're contemplating. He also let me know while he was in your custody, he himself came back and altered the plans for the power unit in the train. It will never work.

"Now to my proof what I have just said to you is actual, factual and true. My proof is in three parts.

"First, in ten minutes you will see an image of Albert appear in this room. That image will be of him as he will look in the year 2045 after being held in isolation for thirty years. You will see he has mutated.

"Second, I will fade out of existence in this room. You and your Chief of Security both saw me, and I shook hands with both of you yet I will be gone and the door will not have been opened. I am sure your Chief is outside the door and I will still leave.

"Third, tomorrow afternoon at exactly one in the afternoon, a man will enter this office and attack you and cut you below your right eye leaving a V shaped scar. Morgan, you will be here no matter what you try or where you go, you will be here in this office and the attack will happen. You will carry that scar the rest of your life.

"The next day after I will come to this office and sit down with you again and we will discuss what I am here for and how you can avoid the terror that will come over the next thirty years. At that time the decision will be yours and you will live or you will die by it."

I had just finished when there was a movement off to my left and as I turned, I could see the image of Albert forming there in the office. Morgan looked over and saw him coming into view. The look on his face was one of absolute disbelief.

He looked at me and then back at Albert. Albert walked over to the desk and stood there looking at Morgan. He then smiled and slowly slipped out of sight.

Morgan looked back at me. "What the hell was wrong with his head?"

"I told you Morgan, during his isolation he got into living within his own mind and as he spent his time in his mind he started to mutate. What you saw was the result of that mutation. That is why he can come here and how he was able to take me through the Time Trap and eventually force me to face my part in the unjust actions taken against him by you.

"Now it's time for me to leave. You will have your experience tomorrow and the next day I will return to this office and we will continue with our discussion."

I stood up and felt myself being lifted up and sliding out of his presence. I found myself back at my car outside of Jack's Bar. I got in my car and headed out of the area. I couldn't go home because I would find myself there with Helen and would only make matters worse. I found a motel and took a room for the night.

The following day the company administration building was crawling with security people. They were loading the place up to protect Morgan. Morgan himself had taken the company jet to the east coast and was holed up at a friend's place.

I sat there in my car across from the building watching what they were doing to cover any unwanted strangers from entering the building. What they didn't know or understand was Albert in 2045 was going to put on a show the likes of which they had never seen.

It was ten minutes to one when I saw the first reaction of the security people at the building. The Chief of Security pulled up in front in his car, got out and ran inside. I knew full well what was happening.

Morgan had moved into his bedroom that night and found he was having a hard time going to sleep. He knew David was out of his head. No one knew where he was and he surely was not in his office on the other side of the continent. He figured he would sit this out until five o'clock and then head back home. He was making special plans for David the next time he saw him.

The next morning, he was up and in the dining room when his friend entered. They greeted one another and then sat down for a light breakfast. They were planning on a day at the golf course and then Morgan's friend would run him to the airport for his flight back home.

They had just finished the first nine holes of the course and were at the bar for a break. He looked at his watch and it was just changing to four o'clock when he felt this sudden jolt and then a flash and he was standing in his office.

Just then the door burst open and a man came charging in at him with a knife in his hand. He was on him before he could react and the blade got him just below the right eye. By then several security people came storming into the office and they subdued the man and hauled him out.

Seconds later his Chief of Security came through the door and stood there looking at him. Morgan was in a state of shock with blood running down his face and over his golf clothes. "How the hell did you get here? I thought you were at Larry's; how did you get here?"

Morgan was holding up his left hand and trying to stem the flow of blood with his right. "I don't know damn-it. I was taking the end of the ninth break when I felt a jolt and here I am. Would you get someone here to take care of this wound?"

I had returned to my motel when I felt a presence. I looked up and Albert was standing there. "David, everything has gone just fine and you've done a great job. How are you holding up?"

"I'm fine Albert, what's our next move?"

"You will go to their office as you said and continue your talk with Morgan. I'm interested in how this has impacted him."

"All right Albert, I'll be there on time and hopefully our little game will result in his changing his mind. By the way, what if he refuses to change his plans, then what?"

He stood there. "We'll cross that bridge when it comes. If he refuses then I have no choice but to go back to my time and kill every one of those bastards. This time I won't stop."

"What about me Albert?"

"David, you've fulfilled your obligation to me. You cannot control what those people do or decide, all you could do is present the situation to them and they have to make the right move. You will return to your place in time and live a good life. My problem is I'll miss you."

I looked at him and nodded my head. "All right Albert, I'll be at the office tomorrow as promised and we'll jerk their chains."

He smiled at me and faded away.

CHAPTER FOURTEEN

Back to the Past

The next day came around faster than I had anticipated. I found myself pulling into the company parking lot at the admin building and parking out and away from the main entrance. I sat there for several minutes knowing I could be walking into a death trap. I didn't know how Morgan had taken his mishap with the stranger. He may be looking for someone he can take his anger out on.

I left the car and walked across the lot and around to the front entrance. As I entered the main lobby the Chief of Security walked up to me. He had me checked for any weapons and then escorted me to the elevator.

Once we were on the elevator, he looked at me. "I don't know how the hell you pulled that game off yesterday, but you didn't change anything."

I looked him straight in the face. "Mister you had better hope I changed something because your life depends on it. Don't take that as a threat from me, it's a statement of fact. If things don't change, you're predestined to die."

We exited the elevator and walked to Morgan's office. As I entered, he was sitting behind his desk with a large bandage on his face under his right eye. "Sit down and let's get on with this."

I sat down and waited for him to say something. Finally, he turned in his chair looking out the window. "All right where do we go from here?"

That was what I wanted to hear. "Then you believe what I told you yesterday and you're willing to address this issue about Albert?"

He was nodding before I had finished and then turned to me. "I was trying to protect the company's rights in maintaining security over our development of the Super Train.

"There is so much at stake here and if any of it gets out then it could destroy us."

"So, you thought depriving a man of his freedom was the right way to go. Did you ever stop to think Albert just may be a loyal and dedicated employee who wanted to see the Super Train Project succeed just as much as you or anyone else?"

"No, I didn't look at it that way. I was concentrating on absolute control and failed to consider the ramifications. My motives were sincere; I just took the wrong path and made the wrong decisions."

"Well Morgan, where do we go from here?"

He stood up and walked over to the window and then turned looking at me. "I'm not sure David. I'm a hardnosed son-of-a-bitch at times and I simply want to control. In this case I pushed it and do you know what, I'm still going to push it."

I knew immediately I was in trouble up to my neck. He stood there looking at me with a contortion to his face only pure anger can create. "You come in here with an attitude you're going to teach me a lesson and then give me three ultimate events and then play that game with me and think I'm going to roll over for you. Well surprise to you, you're full of shit and you're the one who's going to pay."

He then called out and the door burst open and in came the Chief and two of his officers. They walked over to me and jerked me out of my seat. The Chief then came around in front of me and planted his fist right in the middle of my gut. The wind went out of me and I felt myself falling.

They jerked me back up and Morgan walked over to me. "Now you little pig you're going to learn what it means to be loyal. I sure as hell hope your insurance was paid up because if it's not your wife's going to have a hell of a life on her own."

I was still trying to regain my breath when they drug me out of the office and started down the hallway. Morgan was right behind. He continued to talk as they carried me into a service elevator. "You are going to take us to Albert right now. If you don't then I think we will have to include your wife and kids in our actions against you. It's your choice, Albert or your family."

I looked up at him and then over at the Chief. "Albert was right all along. His desire to kill you was well founded. The problem is you don't see every action you take here changes nothing. You're all pre-destined to die and nothing you can do now will change that. Albert made sure of that."

Just then the Chief buried his fist in my gut again sending me to the floor fighting to regain my breath. "Don't play tough guy with me. You don't know what tough is but I'm going to show it to you in just a few minutes. David, you're going to tell us where Albert is one way or the other and then you're going to die.

"You have no idea as to what you have gotten yourself into. I can assure you there is much more involved here than your life is worth. It's nothing compared to what is at stake."

By now I was having a hard time seeing let along hearing his tirade. I was doing everything I could do to keep from throwing up. Morgan stood there looking down on me with this sickening smile on his face.

The elevator reached the bottom and I was drug out and over to another door and through that door into a storage room. Someone turned the lights on and at the same time I landed on my back in the middle of the room.

One of the security officers closed the door and then the four of them circled me. Morgan then leaned over. "Now David, I think you need to start to think your situation over. This is no longer a conversation between two intelligent men. From this point on anything you say will be the difference between the amount of pain you will feel and your final reprieve when we kill you.

"All you have to do is answer my questions truthfully and then we can end this pain. Now where is Albert?"

I started to sit up when one of the officers put his foot in the middle of my chest and pushed me back onto my back. "Answer the question."

"I can't because I don't know. I drove him out of town to the north and let him go."

Morgan stood there shaking his head. "Now David, that's not the truth and you know it. I've been trying to tell you we can end any real pain for you by just telling the truth and then we will send you on your way."

He stepped back and the two security officers started to kick me. They started at my legs and continued up to my chest stopping short of my head. The pain was body wide and deep. All I could do was to try and roll with the blows.

Morgan stepped over to me and bent over. "All right David, you've decided to play hard ball with us and I can assure you these boys know how to play better than you do. Let me ask you again. Where is Albert Aberdeen?"

It was at this point I really knew I was paying for my failure to help Albert in the real time when he had been abducted. I didn't know if Albert would be coming to my aid or I was just going to pay the price.

I lay there trying to decide what I was going to do when I first felt him and then heard him. "No David, I'm not going to abandon you but I am going to let you suffer for a little longer. Not as payback but to let Morgan build in his sense of confidence. Stand by David, its coming."

I looked at Morgan. "Listen to me. Everything you saw and felt the other day was the real thing. That was not me doing it, I was just the messenger. Right now, you have me at a disadvantage and I will agree it hurts.

"I guess the thing you need to know is I have no control over what is happening. In my real time I failed to stand against you when you first abducted Albert. I have been given a second chance and that is why I'm here. In a short time, I will be returned to my real time and you will be facing Albert on your own.

"This time was your opportunity to set things right and you've proven you have no desire to do the right thing. Everything you have done here today will mean the destruction of Grand Futures, INC."

The blow came in low and into my right side. It hit just in front of my right kidney. All I saw were flashes of light and then the pain hit. I felt myself double up and then someone grabbing me and laying me back out on my back.

I couldn't focus on any of them and then the next blow hit on the left side in the same area as it had on the right. I couldn't even scream the pain drove me into shock. It was then I felt another presence.

I started to shake my head and was focusing again when I saw him walk through the wall and into the room. The others saw him and turned toward him, with the three-security people drawing their guns.

Morgan stepped back and around behind the security people. Albert stood there looking at them, "Hi David, you, all right?"

All I could do was nod my head.

Albert looked back at the others. "Put those guns away. You could shoot all day and never touch me."

He stood there waiting for them to holster their guns. After about fifteen seconds he waved his hand and all three guns moved up and each one of the officers turned and pointed their gun at one of the other two so all three was aiming at one of the others.

You could see the fear in their faces as they tried to move the guns. It was then I noticed their trigger fingers were pressing the triggers. The Chief screamed. "Stop, we'll leave and you can deal with Morgan. Just leave us out of it."

All three guns went off at the same time and each in turn dropped to the floor with a single bullet hole in the back of each one's head.

Morgan stood there looking at Albert and then at me and then the three bodies on the floor. He started to move toward the door and the wall on both sides of the door closed turning the room into a door-less room.

Morgan looked like a man lost in a void with no idea as to direction or means of finding his way out. "Albert, you can't be serious. This is all a mistake and I'm sure we can work things out."

"Shut up Morgan, I'll deal with you in a few minutes; right now, I need to deal with my friend David here."

I didn't like the sound of his voice and started to brace myself for the worst. I managed to regain my feet when he turned and walked over to me. As he approached me Morgan was bending down and picking up one of the guns.

Albert waved his hand toward Morgan and the gun slipped out of his hand and all three guns slid across the floor and into the wall.

Albert continued walking toward me. "David, you have been a good friend for many years and when I pulled you into Time Trap I did so with a lot of mixed feelings. On one side I wanted to kill you for not helping me when they abducted me. On the other hand, I understood what you were dealing with and so I decided to give you a second chance.

"So, here we are in this room ready to deal with that animal who did this to me. But I still have feelings toward you and I must deal with them now. I watched as these animals mistreated you and I came to realize you had actually dedicated yourself to this adventure I sent us on.

"My original plan was to kill you along with these others, but I now know you're as much a victim as I was and for that you have earned your freedom.

"David, I'm going to send you back to your time now. You will find yourself at the intersection where Time Trap took you and you will pass through the intersection and then move on to your home and find all as it should be.

"David, I want you to live a good life. But before I let you go you need to know at this time and in this place, I will deal with Morgan and the rest of his administration. You will see the results in the failure of Grand Futures, INC. That will put you out of a job but not for long. You will be hired by a new firm and given a chief engineer's position."

I stood there looking at him. "Albert is it necessary to kill Morgan?"

"Oh David, you never quit do you. Yes, if everything is going to work out right for you and your family and everyone else impacted by this company he and the others must die.

"You will understand when you return to your normal time. Just realize there will be a different history behind you and it will change the future as well. The time you saw thirty years in the future will never develop. It will be replaced by the new future which you will build as you go."

Meanwhile Morgan had been standing there watching and listening. Albert walked up to me and placed his hand on my left shoulder. "Good bye for now David, I'll see you shortly."

At that point my vision started to go light as if someone was shining a bright light in my eyes. The next thing I know I was in my car at the intersection of Fourth and Monroe Street. I stepped on the gas and drove on down the street to my house and pulled into the driveway. It was my house and everything as back to normal.

I could see Helen through the kitchen window working at the sink. I got out of the car and walked up to the back door, turned the door knob and walked in. I was home.

CHAPTER FIFTEEN

Albert's Revenge

Meanwhile back at the storage room in the administrative building one year earlier Albert turned to Morgan. He walked over and stood there in front of him.

Morgan was watching his every move. He couldn't help but be repelled by Albert's appearance. His head was grotesque and he couldn't keep his eyes off of it. "You don't like my head Morgan?"

"Albert I'm not used to it. This is not how you have looked in the past and it is unsettling. Surely, Albert, this is not the result of our holding you at the Sidney complex?"

Albert let Morgan talk as he watched him squirm and try to think of a way out. He was about to change the whole of history in respect to the Grand Futures, INC. That company and all it stood for was about to become a non-existent short stop in times past.

After several minutes Albert reached out and placed his hand on Morgan shoulder. Morgan stopped talking and looked down at Albert's hand. "Mr. Tylor, you have proven to be a rather complex individual. However, there is one thing that is consistent with you and that's the fact you're a bad ass no matter what you're involved in.

"I have now come to the conclusion you can be no other way and that means tomorrow or a thousand tomorrows from now you will be the same and someone would be victimized by you.

"You sir, are a parasite I cannot permit to live. You will only make things worse every moment that you continue to live. I just cannot let that happen, so now I'm in a quandary as to just how I should deal with you.

"I could kill you fast or slow. I think I prefer slow and so that's the way it's going to be. I want you to look this room over carefully. A while back I eliminated the door leaving no way out of this room. If I left you in here in this room alone, that would be one hell of a way to deal with you.

"I have decided to do just that, except for one little change. The interior of this room shall be lined with steel, the walls, the ceiling, and the floor. There will be no way out and no one will ever find you here. Your death will be slow and painful. You'll relive each and every event you have been involved in, the good, the bad, and the mean."

In the flash of a second the steel walls, ceiling and floor came into being. Morgan had a look of total fear and panic wash across his face. "Please Albert; you can't do this to me. Look, I'll guarantee you will never be mistreated by anyone ever. I will guarantee you will be given a top management position. I can make you the lead engineer over the entire Grand Futures, INC.

"Albert, you have to have mercy, no sane man would do what you're planning. Please Albert."

Albert started to fade away as Morgan was pleading for mercy. The last he saw of Morgan was Morgan screaming. "Albert, please for the love of God, don't do this."

Over the next ten hours the upper management team of Grand Futures, INC. started to die out. Every form of accident and illness hit the people in the administration building. In addition, the stocks for the company collapsed which in turn caused the shutdown of all the manufacturing capabilities of the company. In less than a day and a half Grand Futures, INC. was dead and gone.

A year later I was sitting at home when the paper came, I saw the headlines Grand Futures, INC. had collapsed. The company was in receivership and its production lines had died out.

The paper related Morgan Tylor the president and CEO of the company had disappeared without a trace some time earlier. All attempts to locate him ended up in failure as well.

I set the paper down thinking to myself. That's a strange state of affairs I guess I'm out of a job. That probably means the Super Train project is dead as well. I wonder what Albert's going to do.

I picked up the phone and called Albert's home. After the second ring he answered. "Hey Albert, what do you think of the Grand Futures failure?"

"Damn, I don't know David. Looks like were out of our jobs."

"Yeah, I would think so. You have any idea as to what the hell happened?"

"Not sure David, but with Morgan coming up missing he may have cleaned the place out and skipped with all the money."

"What, you really think so?"

"Look David, just about anything could have happened. That's alright with me anyway because I've been working on an idea for my own company. Now. you're out of a job would you consider coming to work for me?"

That caught me by surprise. "Wow, I hadn't thought about that possibility Albert, but if you can use me, I'm ready to go to work for you any time."

"Good David, I'll give you a call in about a week and we'll get things moving. You take it easy for the time being and take your wife out for a good night out while you have the time."

That was it. I had been Time Trapped into the future only to be sent back into the past to correct something I had let slide. Once that correction was made, my life and that of my family was back on track.

It's funny, but I have flash backs of both periods from time to time. I would swear I was dreaming but deep down inside I know it was not a dream. No, it was real and I'm living the results of that time today. As each flash back occurs, I have learned to remember it and take advantage of it in the here and now. It's paid off well, guaranteeing the life my family deserves.

Just a simple run to the post office and thirty years later I'm here right back where I started and living the good life. Did it actually happen? Yeah, I think so.

The new company started by Albert grew by leaps and bounds. It was almost as if Albert knew what was coming or developing in the world of industry. The fact was that he purchased and moved his new company into the old Grand Futures complex.

Three months after Time Trap, INC. obtained the old complex once occupied by Grand Futures; a clerk was moving a number of boxes full of forms into a storage area in the basement.

When she opened the storage room, she found it was full and she started to look around for another room. Over by the elevator she found a door just to the left of the elevator and back in a small inset in the wall.

She checked the door and it was unlocked and she opened it and stepped in and turned on the lights. What she saw sent her running back up to the main security desk in the main lobby.

As she came out of the elevator the security officer saw her stagger out of the elevator and lean against the wall holding her hand to her mouth. He walked over to her. "Lady, are you, all right?"

She looked at him and then started to say something but nothing came out. "Please, Lady you need to calm down and think about what you want to say."

"There are bodies downstairs." That's all she could say.

"Bodies, downstairs, where Lady, where did you see these bodies?"

She grabbed his arm and pulled him into the elevator and when they got to the bottom, she pulled him out and around to the left and to the door. She pointed at the door.

He walked over and slowly pushed the door open and stepped in. There on the floor were the skeletons of four men.

Three still had guns in their hands and the fourth was lying across the top of the other three. He pulled his radio and called the main desk requesting assistance in the basement.

It was five in the afternoon when the police detective walked into my office. "Mr. Jacobs?"

"Yes, that's me."

"Mr. Jacobs, I'm Detective Lewis. May I have a few minutes of your time?"

"Sure Detective, please have a seat."

"Mr. Jacobs, I'm working a case where four bodies were found in a storage room in your basement. Do you know anything or have you heard anything about that?"

"Well yes I have. Our security coordinator came by about eleven this morning and told me there had been four skeletons found in the basement. Have you developed anything, any information as to who they were?"

"Yes, sir we have, and it's almost unbelievable. One of the bodies was that of Morgan Tylor who had been the president of the Grand Futures Company. He had disappeared last year just about this time without a trace.

311

"The other three were his Chief of Security and two of his officers. All three of the Security people had been shot to death. The best we can tell is they shot each other in the head. The bullets from the bodies matched the guns being held by the body behind each one. Sir they all killed each other at the same time.

The last body was Tylor's and it appeared he was in the act of cannibalism when he finally died. What we can't figure out is why he stayed there with those bodies. The door was unlocked and he could have walked out of there anytime he wanted to. The coroner figures he took about five weeks to die."

I sat there looking at him. "Oh my God, how could that happen to a man like Mr. Tylor? We had all thought the he had skipped town when things had gone bad, but it never entered my mind something like this would happen."

"Well, it's a strange one and I don't think we'll ever have an answer for it. We just thought someone should be advised. We're clearing out now and probably won't need that space saved any longer. Sorry for the inconvenience."

"Detective, it was not a problem. We're just sorry something like that happened to those men. They were good men. I just can't figure how it could have happened."

After the detective had left, the side door to my office opened and Albert stepped in. "Funny how someone's guilt can hide the most obvious. All Morgan had to do was walk over to the wall and reach out and grip the door knob and he would have been free.

"But his hate and fear never let his mind search out and find the obvious. That must have been one hell of a way to die."

He smiled and turned and walked back through the door. I closed my eyes and then opened them and continued my life as it was meant to be. The past is the past and only the future can be influenced and built upon.